WITHOUT QUESTION

PAM CHRISTINE

Published 2019 by Creativia (www.creativia.org)

Edited by Elizabeth N. Love

Cover art by Cover Mint

ACKNOWLEDGMENTS

I would like to start by thanking everyone who has been patient in waiting for my book to be published.

I would like to thank my husband Malcolm for his continued support throughout the writing of this book, and for his occasional input with some of the story lines.

I would also like to thank my son Steve for continuing to support me despite the ribbing he has had to take from his friends.

A big thank you to my daughter-in-law Jodie for proof reading my book and offering her valued opinion.

A Special thank you to Sally Hague, a dear friend, aspiring actress and model.
Finally, thank you to Ben Parsons of Take the Scene (www.takethescenephotography.com) for the cover photography.

ABOUT THE AUTHOR

Pamela Christine has written poetry and short stories since she was a child. After reading a well-known erotic book, she decided to try her hand at writing erotic novels. This is her first attempt; Pamela states that she wanted to write something that people could relate to and hopes you will enjoy it as much as she enjoyed writing it.

CHAPTER ONE

I was desperately trying to sleep, not only struggling with the heat, but also the noise from the Adonis and his Greek Goddess in the apartment above us.

I had come away with my husband – just the two of us – to get away from it all. The boys didn't want to holiday with us anymore, preferring the lively action of Ibiza over the peace and tranquillity of Skiathos, somewhere we had holidayed for the past few years.

Just as I thought he had finished, the Adonis was off again; he had the stamina of an Ox, which was saying something in this heat. Her moans were telling me he was good, unless she was just a good actress. It wasn't like I didn't want them to have fun; I just wanted them to move the head board away from the wall to stop that continuous banging. He groaned with passion, while she screamed with pleasure, and I heard one final moan as I drifted off to sleep.

. . .

"What time are we going for breakfast?" I glanced over at my husband. He peered at me over his morning newspaper, his glasses balancing on the edge of his nose.

"It's up to you," he replied, glancing back at his newspaper.

"Ok, shall we go now then?"

With his gaze fixed to his newspaper, James replied "Let's say ten minutes, shall we? I'll finish my coffee and then we'll go."

So why did he say, *It's up to you*?! I rose from my chair and left him on the balcony.

At breakfast I couldn't help but stare at all the couples as they were entering the dining area, curious as to whom the Adonis may be. On reflection, I thought maybe they wouldn't be up yet; after all, they didn't get much sleep – and come to think of it neither did I!

One couple that did stand out were very tactile and constantly smiling at each other, clearly not married. I was unable to understand what they were saying, however; thanks to my basic Greek lessons, I was able to determine that they were not Greek.

He was about six-foot-two and, judging by his olive skin, he obviously tanned easily. He had blue eyes, and his hair was an ash blonde which suggested that he may be Scandinavian. I had no idea really; I was just guessing. His partner was also blonde, nearly as tall and slender. They looked good together. He gently brushed aside the hair from her face and stroked the side of her cheek; she cupped his hand in hers and kissed his palm.

"Anyway, I look at it this way, if Bergan Corporate do

take over the company, we've had it. I mean, where will that leave me? You will have to kiss goodbye to your fancy holidays... are you listening to me, Alex?"

I glanced towards my husband, then back towards the couple. "Yes, dear, and I'd hardly call them fancy."

"I don't think we would get away much. We'd struggle to get one holiday abroad a year, never mind two. Ed seems to think it's a done deal and we'll be out by this time next year." I nodded hoping it was in the right places. "I mean, it's not like I can just get another job, not at my time of life."

I stared back at James. "At your time of life! Good God, James, you're only forty-nine!"

"Forty-nine I might be, but there's not much out there for a management consultant." James noticed I was distracted and followed my gaze.

"Anyway, who are you staring at?"

"I'm not staring, I'm observing. It's the couple who I think are staying above us."

"Oh, not more research. Don't you do enough of that at work?"

"No, not like that." I proceeded to explain to James about the Adonis and his Goddess, and how they kept me awake half the night.

"Well, lucky sod, that's all I can say, I can't remember the last time our headboard saw some action."

Later that day as I lay by the pool reading my book, I began to reflect on my own life and what I had experienced along the way, which, in all honesty, wasn't that much.

I met James when I was nineteen at Nottingham University, where I was studying for a degree in research and development. James was twenty and studying business, with mousy brown hair and hazel eyes. He was tall, six-foot-three inches (to be exact), and lanky with not an ounce of fat on him. I was slim and lacking in breasts, though this did improve slightly after I had the twins. We were both what you would describe as geeks, I suppose, studying day and night for our degrees, which probably explains why we got on so well. I had very little experience in the sex department when I met James, and on reflection neither did he. I'm not saying that we never had sex pre-marriage, but I can honestly say the earth never moved for me, not once.

After four years of studying, we celebrated big style – well, loosely speaking, a couple of bottles of wine and take-away, which was all we could afford. You could say we were evolving rather than falling in love, and on October 26th, 1991, when I was twenty-three, we were married. It had to be then to work it around our jobs, which we were both obsessed with.

Since I was an only child, my Mother wanted to spoil me, insisting I have the best of the best. I wasn't really interested in anything fancy; I just wanted something plain and simple. I eventually got my own way, and although our wedding was only a small affair, it was nice; we were married at St Augustine's Church near my home, which my mother insisted on. James wasn't bothered where it was. A small intimate reception followed at a local hotel, with family and some close friends. Jack was one of them. He was James's best man and a real live wire, a lady's man and cocky with it, so different to James. I remember on our wedding day in the reception line-up, Jack kissed me on my cheek, whilst squeezing my bottom in the process. I was familiar with Jack's advances as I had experienced them a couple of times before. James never knew and still didn't. Not that anything ever happened. I always just laughed them off. Despite that, I constantly felt nervous around him and didn't feel experienced enough to deal with his sexual advances, so I always tried to make sure we were never alone.

On one occasion, Jack and Sarah, his wife, had come around for drinks; they often popped round or we all went out together. I was in the kitchen preparing some snacks when Jack came through. "Need any help?" I turned to look back at Jack. He threw me a cheeky wink like he always did.

"No, I can manage, Jack, thanks." I smiled back at him and turned to face the work surface.

His eyes were a piercing blue and seemed to smile when he did. He always had my stomach doing somersaults. "God your arse looks sexy in those jeans." I blushed as I turned back to face Jack.

"Jack, would you like to take those sausage rolls through for me?" I turned back towards the work surface.

"I'd rather take you."

Before I knew it, Jack was pressed up against me from behind. He moved my hair and his warm lips brushed the nape of my neck, a quiver ran down my spine. I quickly pushed away from him and repeated, "Jack – the sausage rolls. I'll grab the crisps," before making a quick exit into the lounge.

"You ok, hun?" Sarah asked.

"Me? Yes, I'm fine, why?"

"You look a little flushed."

I nervously arranged the various bowls of snacks on the coffee table.

I headed back into the kitchen and called, "It must have been from when I took the sausage rolls out of the oven," laughing as I said it. Things felt a little awkward for me all evening, not that anyone seemed to notice, least of all James. Jack, on the other hand, was not affected in the least and continued to wink and smile at me all evening.

CHAPTER TWO

As the sun went down in Skiathos, James and I took our usual stroll to the bar on the harbour. The traditional Greek blue chairs with wicker seats were always inviting but never very comfy, unless you were lucky enough to get one with a cushion on. We had been going there for so many years. We didn't need to order anymore; there was always a drink waiting for us by the time we got seated at a table. Dimitrious the barman was on first name terms with us and always appeared eager to hear about our day, though he was probably just being polite, as we hardly ever did anything exciting.

"You have a good day today? You have a good tan!" It was certainly coming along nicely. I was starting to blend in with the locals.

"Yes, yes thank you, Dimitrious. We've had a lovely day, haven't we, James?" James was transfixed to the wide-screen TV catching up on the cricket score. "James! I was saying to Dimitrious we've had a nice day."

"Champion! Yes... lovely." His eyes didn't even leave the

screen. To be fair we hadn't really seen much of each other all day; we rarely did. He had been on his laptop in the foyer of the hotel, and I had taken my usual trip to the beach. That was just our usual routine.

That night we got back to the hotel around midnight, had a nightcap, then went up to the room. James was asleep by the time I had finished my usual moisturising routine. I stripped off and slid between the sheets, gently curling my arm around his waist. He grunted some sort of goodnight and turned onto his side, leaving his back facing me. I rolled onto my back and, after some time of kicking the sheet off and pulling it on, I decided I would pour a nice cool drink and sit for a while on the balcony.

Just as I was about to do so, I heard a door close in the apartment above. Their voices seemed to fill the room – it was the Adonis and his Goddess. I listened as a few words were exchanged between them, then everything fell silent. I sighed with disappointment. In a strange way, I was hoping they were going to continue what they started the other evening. Suddenly, I heard a scream and a playful laugh, and I could once again hear soft moans coming from the room above.

More words were exchanged, and the bed started to gently rock to and forth. I imagined his lips gently exploring her body, delicately rolling his tongue over her breasts, playfully biting them and her nipples becoming hard with excitement. I could feel his tongue searching for the indentation of her navel, making his way down to her waiting wet pussy, so hot she was aching. I found myself exploring my own body as the excitement rose in me, my breasts felt full and my nipples hard and erect. I felt so hot, and this time it wasn't the temperature.

My skin felt as soft as satin, smooth and in need of attention. My fingers searched for my clitoris. The area around it was smooth and hair free – it felt good. I slowly inserted my fingers. I was so wet that I slid in deeper, and unexpectedly, I moaned out loud. I could hear she was beginning to pant now, and the headboard was moving to the rhythm of his thrusts. My fingers penetrated deeper and harder. I followed his lead, matching his rhythm, filling with excitement and shuddering with delight. She screamed out as she climaxed. I let out a gentle moan. My body was limp with the rush it had experienced, and I quickly drifted off to sleep.

"So, was the Adonis at it again last night?" James mocked over breakfast.

"I don't know, I was asleep," I replied. I felt myself blush and glanced down towards my coffee cup, nervously continuing to stir it. I was too embarrassed to tell James I had kind of 'got in on the act' and enjoyed it nearly as much as her.

After breakfast I grabbed my book and found a sunbed by the pool. I glanced around to see what everyone was reading. Most of the men were reading fictional war-type thrillers or a newspaper, whilst the women read the latest erotic novels. I glanced down at my book (the latest murder mystery) and wondered if I was missing something. The women in the office had been reading these erotic novels and said I should give them a whirl. Well, maybe I would when I get home.

I must have drifted off to sleep, and I woke with such a jolt I almost leapt off the sun bed. I glanced around the pool area to see if anyone had noticed but appeared to be in the clear. I looked ahead of me across the pool and noticed a cheeky-looking guy looking over at me. Clearly, I hadn't got away with it after all.

He was unshaven, with a white beany hat on, and was chewing on the arm of his sunglasses. He smiled, and I returned the gesture but with a slightly sheepish expression. I wondered what he was doing here alone. I hadn't noticed him before. His partner seemed to appear from nowhere and took her place on the empty bed next to him. Quickly, before she noticed him looking at me, he placed his sunglasses back on and relaxed back onto his bed.

It started to get hot sat by the pool, so I decided to take my usual walk to the beach, to find a quiet spot to relax and read my book. I wandered along the promenade for what seemed like an age before finally finding a sunbed in a peaceful location, with just the sound of the sea lapping against the shore in the background. The bed appeared unoccupied, so I laid my towel down, kicked my sandals off, and lay out. I noticed there was another bed about six feet away with a towel on it, but couldn't see who it could belong to, I figured someone must have reserved it for later. I delved into my book and forgot about the rest of the world. There was no better tonic for me, feeling the sun on my body and listening to the waves gently rolling on to the beach. After a while I turned over on to my front, abandoned my book and just relaxed – something I rarely did back home.

I drifted off to sleep. I wasn't sure how long for, but when I woke up, someone was on the other sun bed. She was tanned with long chocolate brown hair and a body to die for. I placed her around forty. She lay topless on the bed and must have just come out of the sea, as drops of water were still glistening on her breasts. I was mesmerised by her, and as she rolled over onto her front, I quickly looked away in the hope that she hadn't realised I had been staring at her. I waited a while before stealing another look, but this time she looked up and caught my eye. There was no time to look away.

"It's lovely here, isn't it, so peaceful." She had a deep velvet voice that carried a strong accent.

"Yes, erm... well, I've never actually been to this side of the beach before."

"I come here all the time... I'm Maria, by the way."

"I'm Alexandra, well, Alex. Pleased to meet you."

"So, have you not been to Skiathos before, Alex?" she asked.

"Oh, yes, we've been coming for years. I've just never been to this side of the beach."

"It's the best side, in my opinion, so relaxing. I come here every day to relax and swim. I have a place near here, just a small shack, I guess."

"Oh, that's nice. So do you live here or just rent somewhere?"

"I live here, been here about ten years now."

"Are you not from Greece then?"

"Yes, I'm Greek but from the mainland."

"Oh, I see. You speak good English."

"Thank you. I lived in London for eight years and managed to pick it up while I was there."

Maria and I chatted like we had known each other for years. I discovered she was married and had two children. She had previously been a designer, producing clothing which was sold internationally, and now she made a humble living offering massages, using various methods including aromatherapy. Maria said she managed to make enough money to live on in Skiathos, and I could see the attraction.

Skiathos was such a green island and still tourist free in certain areas. I loved it here and hoped I would also get the chance to make a home here one day. I was fascinated by her stories and could have listened to her all day. I began to tell her about how stressful my job was and about James's job.

"You could use one of my massages." We both laughed.

"Yes... yes, I guess I could."

I was feeling dehydrated and reached for my bottle of water, which by now was lukewarm, and I shuddered as I drank it.

"Is there a bar nearby, Maria?"

"No, I'm afraid not. That's what I like about it here, it's as far away from tourists as you can get." I could see her point. "I can fix you a drink at my place if you want?"

"That would be nice, thank you."

Maria slipped her bikini top back on and threw her towel over her shoulders. I jumped up quickly and slipped my sandals on, grabbed my things and followed. We continued to chat with hardly a pause – just like old friends.

CHAPTER THREE

We soon reached Maria's shack (as she called it). It was lovely, with a small decked area that had a couple of sun loungers on it. A shell mobile hung from a canopy, which provided a shaded area that was perfect for this time of day.

Maria beckoned me into the room. "Take a seat." I sat down on the wicker couch, which was well worn but cosy. The "shack" was well-named, with bare wooden floor boards and oak beams. Family photos were scattered here and there. I picked up a photo of a couple.

"My kids – Sofia and Christos."

"Aww, they're lovely."

"Thank you! Sofia is at university in Athens and Christos is doing his military service."

Maria poured me a chilled glass of white wine and proceeded to tell me about her life. She was married, but her husband worked away as a contractor. I naively thought all Greeks were fishermen. I began to giggle out loud and had to confess to Maria what I had thought.

"Ah, Stavros' father was a fisherman," said Maria. "Stavros broke the chain."

We chatted for about an hour. I told her about our boys and what they were doing back home. Life was so different here. Moving onto a second bottle of wine, we giggled like teenagers as we talked about our life experiences. Then Maria got up and walked towards the door. "Come, you need a massage." I looked across at her. "I won't charge you full price." She winked; we both laughed.

I made my way towards the door she had gone through. I was feeling quite light-headed, and the wine had taken its toll.

"I have different essential oils I can use," Maria offered as she showed me into the bedroom. An old wrought-iron bed was the focal point of the room, with crisp white sheets that looked as though they had been ironed into place. White shutters graced the windows and were slightly ajar, allowing a warm and gentle breeze to blow through, making the curtains dance softly.

Maria laid a soft white bath towel on the bed and asked me to lay face down. Without question, I nervously did as she asked. She unhooked my bikini top and slipped it off my arms. I could smell the Jasmine oil as she ran it through her fingers. She sat astride me, and her fingertips touched my neck, sending a quiver through my body.

She gently worked her way down my back, stroking it with her palms, whilst her thumbs and fingertips worked in deep circles down my body. She lightly grabbed and lifted my muscles, and it felt so good that, for a moment, I couldn't breathe.

Maria's hands were like silk, caressing me... arousing me. Her fingers were searching my body, and I could feel her long hair gently brushing against my skin as she moved. Her hands explored every part of my tingling body, right down to my toes. She slowly began to make her way back up my waist and slipped two fingers into the top of my bikini pants. I breathed deeply into the pillow as she slowly began to pull them down over my thighs.

As she moved back up my legs, her hands kneaded deep into my skin, pushing hard against my thighs, moving up and down. Maria began to work further up my body, and it was then I had noticed she had removed her bikini top. When? I don't know. All I knew were her warm breasts were brushing against my back, her nipples erect and hard, and I was so turned on.

Part of me wanted to leap off the bed and escape, but the rest of me was curious, wondering what Maria had planned. She moved the hair from the nape of my neck and kissed it softly. An unexplainable shock ran through my body, and she whispered in my ear with her unmistakable sexy voice, "Turn over." I froze, wondering what to do. It felt wrong but, on the other hand, so right. She repeated again, "Turn over, please."

I gathered my thoughts. I was mistaken. Maria didn't want me; my imagination had been running wild. I rolled over on to my back and she remained astride me, gently manipulating my body, shoulders, stomach, legs and then my breasts, which were full with excitement. I let out a groan.

"Hush," Maria whispered, "hush." She began to kiss my body slowly, playfully biting my breasts whilst I just lay there unsure whether to respond or not.

"Do you not want to play, Alex?" Maria asked. I looked up at her, holding her gaze. Our lips met, her mouth felt as soft as velvet, and she moaned as we suddenly locked together, rolling around on the bed. I explored her breasts with my tongue. She was so soft and warm. I had never felt this way with James and her gentleness was so sensual.

Her hands began exploring my body again, her fingers slowly working their way between my thighs. She pushed them inside me, and the rush I felt was amazing, almost electric.

I could feel my clitoris throbbing, yearning for more, and my heart was pumping so loud I could hear it beating. Maria began to passionately kiss me again, her lips left mine as she began to move slowly down my body, her tongue exploring every inch of me. She gently parted my legs and her warm lips kissed me, her tongue pushing hard against my clitoris, darting in every direction. I shuddered with excitement. Every part of my body seemed to be pulsating. Then I felt a rush, causing my back to arch. I yelled, "No... no!" When really I meant "yes!"

I climaxed like never before. The bed felt wet beneath me. I gave out a large sigh and my whole body completely relaxed. I lay still afterwards, my whole-body tingling.

Maria looked up at me and asked, "Alex, are you ok?"

"Yes, why?"

"Because you didn't speak for a while."

"I'm fine."

The truth was I couldn't speak as I felt numb, not in a bad way, but in an unusual way – I had never felt like this before. I lay in Maria's arms for a while, silent and not knowing what to say. I could still hear the sound of the waves crashing against the shore. It felt so tranquil and perfect.

After what seemed like a few minutes, I glanced at the bedside clock. It was just after five. I couldn't believe it. James would be wondering where I was. I leapt off the bed, causing Maria to jump up. "Is everything ok? What's wrong?"

"Nothing, nothing's wrong. I have to go. I didn't know what time it was."

I scrambled to get dressed. Maria wrapped a towel around herself and asked, “Have I upset you?”

“No, no, Maria, you haven’t upset me, honestly. I just have to go.” I slipped my sandals on, tied my sarong around my waist and turned to Maria. “Thanks, Maria. Thanks for the drinks and the... Well, anyway, thank you.” Maria looked back at me confused as I turned and made my way to the door.

CHAPTER FOUR

The walk back to the hotel seemed to take forever, although it was probably only about twenty minutes. My head was all over. What had I done? What possessed me? This wasn't me, what was I thinking? I knew one thing: I couldn't answer any of these questions.

I walked into the hotel foyer; no James. I made my way back to the room and found him laid on the bed sleeping. I tried to close the door quietly behind me, but the catch clicked as I closed it. James stirred and rose his head off the pillow. Rubbing his eyes, he called out, "Oh, you're back then. I thought you had gotten lost."

I went to sit on the bed next to him. "No, I fell asleep on the beach, couldn't believe it when I woke up."

"Tut-tut. Hope you had plenty of sun cream on." I smiled back at James and went through to the bathroom.

"I'll just take a shower," I called through.

I turned the shower on and sat on the toilet, going through everything in my mind that had happened that afternoon. I don't know how long I had been in there, but I was startled by James shouting.

"Come on, you've been ages. What are you doing?"

"Nothing. I'll be out in a minute." I jumped into the shower and immersed my head under the warm spray. Closing my eyes, I thought again about the events that had unfolded. I could still feel Maria's hands gently exploring my body and her warm breath as her lips brushed my skin. "Alex!" I jumped as James called me again. I grabbed a towel, wrapped it round my hair and made my way into the room.

"'Bout time. Bloody hell, you'll wash yourself away."

"Sorry, it's all that sand, it gets everywhere."

The next morning when I woke, it all seemed like a dream; I couldn't believe I had done what I had. It wasn't like me at all. A shudder ran down my spine. I couldn't tell if it was through excitement at what had happened or fear of what I had done. James came in from the balcony. "You slept well last night, hardly a peep out of you, no tossing and turning."

Hmm, was that contentment or the fact that I was exhausted after Maria had finished with me? Well, which ever it was, I was unable to explain it to James.

"Oh, well, I usually fall into a sleeping pattern just before we are due home," I called to James as he wandered back onto the balcony. I grabbed my phone and texted my best friend Sally.

Hi Sal, not sure what's happened to me, but my world has turned upside down! :-/ xxx

I sent the message, grabbed my bag, and we headed off for breakfast. James headed straight for the food. I grabbed a table and, while I waited for him to return, I received a message back from Sal.

Jeez Alex, what's happened? X

Really can't say Sal, just that we NEED to meet for a coffee and a chat when I get home x

For God's sake Alex, that's two days away! Has James lost his job? Are you pregnant? x

Hell no! I'm not pregnant and James' job is OK I think… Trust me, it's not something I can text, but I'll see you soon x

Sally continued to text me back throughout breakfast, reeling off question after question. I just told her all would be explained.

We took time out that afternoon and visited our usual bar on the seafront. Dimitrious was there and started to prepare our drinks at the bar as we approached. I had my usual vodka and lemon, whilst James had his whisky and dry, both drinks cooled with a couple of cubes of ice. We took a seat at our usual table with the old, blue, wooden chairs overlooking the beach.

"So anyway, Ed's been in touch via email this morning, and he reckons that there may be some sort of break-through, and that Bergan may be pulling out." *Oh Hallelujah!* I thought to myself.

"Oh, well, that's good news then."

"My thoughts exactly. I'm going to contact Geoff this afternoon to find out the final outcome."

At that point Dimitrious arrived with our drinks. "You have a good day today?"

"Yes, just the same old thing you know, breakfast, beach and chilling."

"Oh damn," I scorned. "I meant to collect that plate from that little gift shop for your mother." James's mum had a collection of Greek plates we had brought her over the years. I had intended to catch the bus earlier, but it went clean out of my head with everything that had happened to me.

"Would you like me to take you?" Dimitrious asked.

"No, it's fine. I couldn't put you to any trouble."

"No trouble! I finish at three, we can go then. It will take no time on my bike."

"Well, if you really don't mind." Although, the thought of going on a bike filled me with fear. The last time I had been on one was when I was nineteen. Jack had a Yamaha when we were at Uni and he took me for a spin one day. I hated it. It was more like being on the wall of death, he showed off tearing around on it, not my scene at all.

James was fidgeting for the next hour, constantly talking about how his job may or may not change, whilst I looked out to sea and sipped my third vodka and lemon, dreaming of another life I could be living. Suddenly James rose from his seat.

"Ok, well, I really must go, got to make the call." He finished the last of his whisky and headed back to the hotel, his flip flops slapping against his feet as he went.

I grabbed my drink and wandered over to the bar, hitching myself up on a bar stool.

"I finish soon, half-hour I'll be ready."

"It's fine, Dimitrious, no hurry."

"One more drink while you wait, on me." Dimitrious poured me another drink, which I was not sure was a good idea as I already felt light-headed. I watched him tending the bar and its customers, always smiling and not a care in the world, unlike James always droning on like he had the weight of the world on his shoulders. I suppose that seemed a bit harsh under the circumstances. I realised he was conscious that he may not have a job to go home to and it must be a great weight on his mind.

James had put a lot of extra hours in over the years, working into the night. Maybe I was a being unfair. I looked out to sea and wished I didn't have to go home to my humdrum life back in England. Everything was always so much more relaxed here. Maybe if James did lose his job that's what we should do, move out to Greece. The pace was so much slower there, nothing was rushed, and everyone was so friendly. I loved the sights and sounds of the harbour; it was so tranquil.

Just then Dimitrious called out to me – "Two minutes." I looked up and nodded. He had the most beautiful chocolate brown eyes. I smiled across at him thinking my mother would have called them 'come to bed eyes.' They were deep, passionate and sexy. I suppose the events the day before had made me take further stock of my life.

"Okay, shall we go?" Dimitrious startled me.

"Erm, yes," I replied. I quickly finished my drink and followed him to the bike, which looked like it had seen better days. "Erm, have you got a helmet?" I asked. Dimitrious turned and laughed. "No, no helmet. I am a good driver, you need no helmet." I looked at the machine before me with its well-worn seat and shabby paint work, which displayed more rust than paint, and I hoped it would bring me back safe.

Dimitrious straddled the bike, removing his white, tight fitting t-shirt in the process and securing it round his waist. His bronze torso was perfect in every way. He kicked the bike off and signalled me to get on. I climbed on in anticipation, wrapping my arms around his waist.

"Hold on," he called, and we were off.

The breeze that kissed my skin as we made our way up the mountain was warm and tender. Only wearing my bikini top, the naked areas of me pressed against Dimitrious' hot silk skin, and this made me feel wanting in more ways than one. If Dimitrious had stopped and seduced me, I can't say I would have resisted. Maria had unleashed passions in me I had never felt before.

As we made our way up to the village, the familiar chorus of the crickets filled the air. We rode for about half-an-hour before we reached our destination. The main street of the village was lined with quaint gift shops and old-world café bars.

I signalled to Dimitrious to pull over when I spotted the relevant shop, almost falling over trying to get off the bike, giggling like a teenager. I think it was that extra vodka and lemon.

I rushed into the tiny shop in the hope of getting served quickly, which was a mistake. No one gets in and out of a shop quickly in Greece. They love to pass the time of day with you, and everyone is so friendly.

"Hello, my friend, how are you?" Larissa was Stavros' mother; he was the owner of the shop. She clasped my hands and kissed me on both cheeks. “You have come for plate for your mama?”

“Yes, please, can you choose one for me?”

“Where is James?”

“Oh, he’s back at the hotel, busy with work as usual.”

“Ok, I see him next time, I make good for plane journey and pack well.”

She was so sweet, and nothing was too much trouble. “That will be lovely, thank you.” I just didn’t want to be hanging about too long as I didn’t want to put Dimitrious out any more.

While she finished wrapping the parcel, we chatted about the children, whom she hadn’t seen for a long time, and I explained to her that they were no longer children. Eventually the plate was wrapped I hugged Larissa and made my way out of the shop. I need not have worried about Dimitrious as he was passing time talking to the locals. “Ok, you ready to go?”

I nodded, waving the package in my hand, signalling that I had got what I came for. It was just as well that Larissa had packaged it well, as I had to hold on to it with only one hand on the journey back to the hotel, as I needed the other one to hang on to Dimitrious.

We travelled back down the mountain following the winding road, shaded by the olive and lemon trees. It was lovely. The smell of citrus filled the air and I felt good. I leaned into Dimitrious as he turned the corners, and I longed to tell him to carry on and not stop. I was feeling free and enjoying the ride. I didn’t want it to end.

CHAPTER FIVE

We were due to fly home the next day. I had packed most of our things the night before, and so there wasn't much to do. We had breakfast and James said he was going to check out how things were going with work. I couldn't just sit around all day as I hated waiting to leave; it was the worst feeling in the world. We never seemed to get early flights, and they were always late. I guess that's what made them cheaper.

I told James I was going to have one last wander around the resort. I strolled down the main street, in and out of the many shops I had been in before. Before I knew it, I was heading for the beach, to the spot that I had met Maria, but there was no sign of her. She must have gone for lunch or something – or maybe she was giving another massage. I sat for a moment on the sun lounger where we had previously met. As I looked out to sea, I thought about my time with Maria, wondering what her life was really like. I guess that was something I'd never know.

. . .

In a strange way, I felt disappointed that I was unable to say goodbye to her. I suppose I felt awkward having to leave the way I did. I hoped she would understand, my head was so mixed up, but I couldn't hang around for much longer. James would be having a fit. I returned to the hotel and grabbed myself a coffee and a sun lounger to catch the last few rays of sun before I had to leave.

I was left with that same gut feeling that I always had when it was home time: I wished I could stay. I was not looking forward to returning to work. My colleagues Lily and Susan would be sat at their desks busy dissecting everybody and everything. Research was so boring to me now. I did not get the same buzz out of it that I used to get. In fact, one thing this holiday had taught me was that I was not getting much of a buzz out of life at all.

I must have dropped off to sleep because the next thing I remember is James calling me.

"Come on, we need to grab the cases, the coach will be here soon."

"Yes, I'm coming."

I sat up, gathered myself together, slipped my sandals on and followed him back to the room. One last check of the room drawers, cupboards, etc., and a check of the balcony, which gave me a last look of the view. Nothing could beat it, and I would be back here at the first chance I could get.

We made our way out the door, and just as I was making my way down the stairs, I heard the door close from the apartment above us. It was the Adonis and his Goddess. I needed to see what they looked like.

I made an excuse to James that I needed to go back to the room to check something and as I turned to head back up the stairs I came face to face with the Adonis. He was wearing a Stetson, white socks and sandals, was quite stocky (some might say fat) and probably in his mid-sixties. The Goddess was directly behind him, of similar age and build, neither living up to the image I had in my mind. I managed a smile as I passed them and hurried back up to the apartment, giggling to myself as I went in.

Well, life certainly isn't all you imagine it to be sometimes! I hurried back to James who was impatiently tapping his foot at the hotel foyer.

"Come on, hurry up, the coach will be here soon."

I handed the key to Anna the receptionist.

"Thank you, Mrs Whelan, see you next time."

"Thanks again, Anna. Yes, see you soon!" Just as we stepped out, the coach pulled up. "There you go, that was good timing," I called to James.

"Huh? Only just made it, you mean."

James was back on his laptop the minute we got on the coach. I think he was glued to it most of the time. There was only an hour transfer to the airport, but it felt like longer, and the numerous pickups and horrendous queues to check in made time drag even more. One good thing is that there were no delays with the flight, and eventually we were on the plane. I got as comfy as I could and fell asleep.

We arrived back to an empty house around 10.30pm. The boys would be clubbing somewhere no doubt.

"I at least thought they would have had a bit of a tidy."

"Why? They never have before."

James was right. I guess I would have thought something was wrong if they had. I carried my bag upstairs, had a quick shower and climbed into bed. I didn't hear James come up to bed, but I heard the boy's come in around 4am, and then I drifted back off to sleep.

The Sunday papers arrived as usual the next day; I had ordered them to be delivered on our return. I sat in the conservatory with my coffee and copy of *The Times*, looking out onto the garden and wishing I was back in Skiathos with my much-preferred view of the mountains. My phone beeped; it was Sal.

Hi, are you home? Are you even up? When can we meet? Xx

Hi Sal, yes, we're home, not sure when really – maybe tomorrow night after work? X

Oh, hell Alex, you're gonna make me wait that long!? X

Sorry, it's the only free time I've got, and I'm shattered today. See you tomorrow about 8pm at The Wine Cellar on Main Street xxx

Ok, see you then. Hope you are ok xxx

The rest of the day passed pretty quickly. The boys didn't rise till mid-afternoon, and I had done most of the holiday washing by then. I sorted my outfit for work the next day and ironed a shirt for James, settling down with a glass of wine and an hour in front of the TV before I retired to bed.

. . .

I was busy at work the next day trying to catch up and hardly had chance to recall my experience on holiday.

"Did you have a good holiday, Alex?" Lily called out as I passed her desk.

"Yes, thanks, it was lovely, didn't want to come home."

"Oh, you never do."

Which was true. I glanced back at Lily just in time to catch her giving Susan that knowing look.

"So, did you do anything exciting?" Lily asked.

"No, not really," I replied, hoping I could hide my blushes.

"Well, I could do with a week away myself, couldn't you. Susan?"

Susan nodded in agreement and continued to type. I couldn't do for anymore digs from Lily, so I decided to go and make myself a cup of coffee.

When I returned to my desk, I began to daydream about the day I met Maria. It all seemed surreal, so much so I couldn't believe it had happened. I was interrupted by my phone as a message came through.

Hi Alex, are we still on for tonight? x

Yep still on! See you at 8! X

That got me thinking, how was I going to explain to Sal about all this? Sal was a broad-minded soul with a colourful life, married twice, now divorced and currently living the high life. But this was something she would never expect to hear from me.

The day passed by relatively quickly which I was pleased about, I always hated my first day back at work. I was able to get showered and changed into something more casual at work and caught a taxi on to Main Street. I arrived at The Wine Cellar about 7:50pm. Sal was already there, with a chilled bottle of wine and two glasses at the ready. She frantically waved across the room at me, dressed to kill as usual with not a single long, blonde hair out of place.

"So, spill the beans," Sal begged.

"God, Sal let me get my coat off!"

I had known Sal a long time, after meeting on a bus we used to share to work. It started by saying morning to one another and then we ended up sharing our life stories, meeting for coffee and nights out. She always managed to turn heads. She and James shared the same sense of humour and enjoyed some cheeky banter whenever their paths crossed. I didn't mind; it was all harmless fun.

"So, what's happened, Al? What was so bad you couldn't text it to me?"

I began to tell her about my day on the beach with Maria, her jaw dropping wider and wider the longer I continued. It was quite funny, really, as she wasn't easily shocked.

"Oh my god, Alex, what the hell! That's not like you! Was she good?" She fired a barrage of questions at me, which, in all honesty, most of them I couldn't answer. "So, what brought this on, had you and James been arguing?"

"No, not really. I don't know why it happened, I really don't. I was just as shocked as you are."

"So, are you going to see her again?"

“Hell, no, Sal, it was... well, just a one off."

We spent the night going over and over it, laughing at some of it and how I was in disbelief at it happening. Then Sal said, "I don't know why you’re getting so wound up about it. I've done it."

"You haven't!"

"Of course, and on more than one occasion too."

"What! Well, when?"

"Well, the first time was at sixth form. I had a sleepover at a girlfriend’s, her parents were away. We had a few glasses of wine and scared ourselves silly with horror movies. By the end of the night we decided we would share her parents’ double bed, and it kind of just happened. We were just in our bra and knickers, got into bed, and she hugged me saying she had enjoyed the night. Then out of the blue, she kissed me. I just froze and didn’t know what to do. She must have seen this in me and asked me, ‘Do you fancy some strawberries and cream?’

“Of course, I said yes. She asked me to wait there and, in no time, she was back upstairs with a large bowl of strawberries and a tin of squirty cream. We were both giggling. I went to grab a strawberry from the bowl. ‘Oh no you don’t, you have to take it from me.’ She popped the strawberry into her mouth, just biting the edge of it. I bent forward and bit a piece of strawberry. ‘No, like this,’ she said, placing the strawberry between my teeth. She went to bite the strawberry from me, ate it, and continued to explore my mouth with her tongue. I was so turned on it felt amazing, I lay down and she was on top of me, clamping her mouth over my breast. She reached for the cream and covered her nipples on each breast with it.

“‘Do you want some?’ She pushed her breast towards my

face; I didn't know what to do, I just laughed at her. 'Come on... try it'

"I looked up at her and slowly, gently licked around the areola of the breast. Working my way towards her nipple, my lips folded around her breasts. She pushed me down onto the bed and covered me in cream, adding strawberries and then spent the next few minutes eating them off me. You can imagine where she ran her tongue over my body. We were sliding together all over on the bed, and it was amazing."

"Christ, stop it, Sal, you're turning me on."

Sal laughed. "That's just the tip of the iceberg. I could make your hair curl."

"Bloody hell, what else have you done?"

We sat and chatted for hours, and Sal told me about some of her sexual experiences. I was fascinated; suddenly my experience wasn't so unusual. I arranged to have a night out with her a couple of weeks later and made my way home.

CHAPTER SIX

The following weekend, Jack and Sarah came around for a drink. James wanted to tell Jack about how his job was safe and the new ideas he had.

"Looking good, Alex."

"Thanks, Jack," I answered, blushing as usual.

"Did you two have a good time?" Sarah asked.

"Yes, thanks, Sarah. It was lovely." I wandered into the kitchen to fix the drinks and she followed me through.

"So, what did you get up to, anything good?"

"No, not really. Well, we just did our usual, just chilled out."

"Huh, at least you got away. I think Jack has gone off holidays. All he's interested in is work and his secretary."

"Aww, I'm sure that's not the case," I replied back to Sarah, knowing full well it would be.

"Well, I guess Jack is just Jack. I'll never change him." We grabbed the drinks and made our way back to the lounge. James was still droning on about work; Jack was used to him and took it in his stride.

. . .

Later that night, I headed into the kitchen to pour some drinks and Jack followed me in. "Did you miss me then, Al?"

"Didn't really have time to, Jack." The wine had relaxed me, and I gave him a cheeky wink and a smile.

"Liar, you know you have." Jack moved towards me in the kitchen. "You know it's only a matter of time before it happens, Al."

"And what's that, Jack?"

"I think you should think carefully about it."

Just then, Sarah walked in. "Think carefully about what, Jack?"

"About moving house. I think it's about time they had a change. They've been here since they had the boys."

"God, Jack, I can't believe you are touting for business from our friends."

"Well, you know me, always on the prowl." Jack glanced across at me, grabbed his and James's drink, and headed back into the lounge.

"Hmmm, don't I just," Sarah mumbled. I quickly made my way over to the fridge to grab another bottle of wine and pretended I hadn't heard her.

"So, how's work going, Sarah?"

"Oh, not bad I guess, could be better."

"Well, we all think that, don't we? I'd be quite happy not to work at all."

"What, so you can move to Greece?"

"Yes, I'd go tomorrow if I could."

And I meant it. I would if only I got the chance.

. . .

The following Monday, Sal rang me and asked if I fancied a night out on Friday. "Yeah, why not, where do you fancy?"

"Not bothered really, anywhere."

"Ok then, Sal, let's go into town."

We met up on the Friday, and in no time, we were back on the usual subject. "So, what are these stories to make my hair curl?"

Sal laughed and replied, "I wondered when you would ask. I'm not sure you would be impressed."

"Well, I don't know about that, but I am intrigued."

Sal began to tell me about a club she visited on a regular basis called Secret Dreams, a place open to everyone married or single, something I would probably call a pleasure house. "What the hell, Sal, where is this place based?"

"It's about thirty minutes away."

"Really!"

"Yeah, it's a large house, members only."

"And you are actually a member, Sal?"

"Of course, fully paid up." She grinned.

"So, what goes on there?"

"All sorts, bondage, swapping, and voyeurism – you name it, it happens."

"You're having me on. Are you really a member?"

"Yeah, why not?"

"So, how long have you been going?"

"Around six months."

"What, every week?"

"No, I don't go every week. It's every other Friday."

"And is it full on sex or what?"

"Sometimes, yeah. It depends what you fancy and who

you meet. There are all walks of life there. Lawyers, doctors, solicitors, judges, etc."

"What about health risks?"

"Oh, trust you, Alex!"

"Well, I can't help it. It's the first thing that entered my head, and don't you ever worry about it?"

"Well, yes, but that's part of the club thing. It's all about ensuring that you are safe."

"But surely, Sal, there are no guarantees."

"Hey, there's no guarantees in life at all."

"True, but I think I would be concerned about the risks."

"Well, that's as may be, but I'm quite comfortable with everything the way it is."

We sat chatting about Sal's club meetings till the early hours, and I learnt a lot about my friend. "Why don't you come with me, Alex?"

I stared back at Sal in disbelief. "What, me!?"

"Why not? I can introduce you to it and see what you think, and it's free the first time. If you like it, you pay three hundred pounds for the membership and then twenty-five pounds every time you go."

"Hmmm, so it's not cheap then."

"Of course not, it's an exclusive club."

"I don't know, Sal, I'm not sure it's really me. I would have to think about it. The wildest thing I've ever done only just happened in Skiathos."

"I know, Alex, and nobody's twisting your arm. All I'm saying is give it a go. It's exciting and you can just watch. There's no pressure."

"I'll think about it."

. . .

That night I hardly slept at all. I couldn't believe Sal was going to a place like that. I really couldn't get my head round it. I was horrified and yet intrigued at the same time.

The next day I called Sal and asked her when the next night at Secret Dreams was being held. "It's a week on Friday." I then asked if there was any dress code. "No, just sexy but tasteful. Are you coming then, Alex?"

"Possibly," I replied.

"Ooooh, get you."

I laughed down the phone. "I've still got nearly two weeks to change my mind."

"If you do, you'll be sorry! I've got to go anyway. I'm a bit busy at the mo. Speak soon, bye," and with that she was gone.

I spent every spare minute of the next few days looking for something tasteful yet sexy. It drove me mad. Too big, too small, tarty, you name it, I called myself it as I tried on an abundance of outfits. I had given up and had decided to just wear my little black dress, which always seemed to be a hit with Jack. Then again, I suppose anything was a hit with him.

I left work at 3.30 on the Friday and headed for the park-and-ride to collect my car, apprehensive about what the night would hold for me.

As I hurried along, something caught my eye in a shop window. Red, fitted, and very sexy, just plain, but I was sure I could finish it off with accessories. In the changing room, I slipped straight into the dress. It was like it was made for me.

I couldn't believe my luck. It made me feel sexy and confident, and suddenly I was excited about the whole thing.

I arrived home around 5:30 and prepared tea. Wouldn't it be nice if I came home and it was all done for me – that was never going to happen.

We all sat down together, something I liked to make sure we did at least once a week so we could all catch up and talk to each other. Most of the time the boys were in their rooms on games consoles and James was with his best friend, the laptop.

"Mum, could you give us a lift into town tonight?" Josh asked.

"I'm afraid not."

"No!? Why?"

"You'll have to ask your Dad. I'm going out."

"Where are you going?" They both asked together.

"Just going out with Sal for a drink."

"But you went out with her a couple of weeks ago," Jake protested.

"Oh, well, that's just not good enough is it, two nights out in two weeks."

"Well, no, Mum, it's not that. It's just that you don't normally go out that much."

"Exactly, and I work hard, so I think I deserve the odd night out." James just carried on eating his tea, oblivious to it all, no doubt his mind was wrapped up in work.

"So, Dad, can you drop us off in town?"

"Don't see why not. Do you want a lift too, Alex?"

"Depends what time you're going. I'm meeting Sal at 7:30."

"Aww, no, Mum, we're not meeting the lads till about 9:30." James looked up from his plate.

"9:30! That's a bit late to be going out isn't it?"

I interrupted the conversation. "It's ok, I'll make my own way there." I got up from the table and left them discussing the pros and cons of going out early and late.

I popped in the shower and again began thinking about the night ahead, wondering if I should go or not. I slipped into my dressing gown while I dried my hair and drank a couple of glasses of wine in the process. I took my black lace bra and matching thong from the drawer. I think I had only worn it once before. The minute I put the dress on, I got that feeling again. I felt sexy. I didn't feel the need to wear tights as my legs were still tanned from our holiday.

Matching black jewellery and black stilettos finished the look. I felt ready to go. I booked a taxi to collect me straight away. I didn't even mention it to James again; he would have only moaned, and it wasn't worth it. The taxi blew his horn as I was just putting the last few things in the dishwasher. I shouted bye to everyone as I left but didn't get a reply.

CHAPTER SEVEN

When I reached the wine bar, Sal was already there (as usual). She looked stunning in a short black dress and seamed stockings with her hair pinned up.

"Wow, look at you," I said.

"Well now, I could say the same. You don't scrub up so bad yourself!" We both laughed.

"Cheeky Sod."

"Aww, I'm only joking, Alex. Are you excited?"

"Erm... mixed emotions. I suppose it's the thought of the unknown."

"Well, don't worry. I hope it meets your expectations. It might not be what you were thinking..." And what was I thinking, I didn't know, I hadn't a clue. I'd never been to anything like this before. I was probably the most inexperienced person around.

We sat and chatted for a while. I was gulping wine like someone waiting to go on a blind date. My stomach was doing somersaults and I felt sick. I mentioned to Sal how apprehensive I was.

"Oh, Alex, you'll be fine! Just treat it like a night out, meeting new friends. Have a dance, relax and enjoy yourself."

"Oh, right, so you can dance?"

"Look, I think it might be best if we get off now... then you can see for yourself."

Sal phoned a taxi, and it was outside within minutes. I think we were then travelling for about twenty or thirty minutes, during which we didn't speak much at all. I was staring out of the window trying to work out exactly where we were going.

We came off the main road and followed a narrow country lane, then turned onto the start of what appeared to be a long driveway and found ourselves in front of some very large gates. The taxi driver got out of the cab and pressed a buzzer to the side. Words were exchanged – I couldn't hear what – and the driver got back in whilst the gates opened.

"This is a bit cloak and dagger, isn't it, Sal?" It reminded me of a film or something.

"Stop panicking, its fine."

We drove for a short while, then came to what I could only describe as a stately home. Sal paid for the taxi, and we made our way up to the door. My heart was pounding so hard I thought it would leap out of my chest. Sal rang the bell, and a tall, handsome guy opened the door.

"Good evening, Miss Preston, are you well?"

"Very well, thank you, Adam."

The entrance was amazing, with large statues of naked men and women, marble floors, a winding staircase and six doors that lead off from the entrance. I could hear music in the distance; Adam showed us through the first door which I was assuming was the main hall.

It was just like entering any other club. There was a bar to the left with a very dishy cocktail waiter, and tables placed around the room. The dance floor took up the middle of the room and the lighting was low, creating a very seductive atmosphere. The music seemed to hover around the eighties and nineties which suited me down to the ground.

We made our way over to the bar, and I was starting to feel quite relaxed. It wasn't at all what I was expecting. Sal seemed to know a lot of people (mostly men) and was having brief chats with them as we passed. I couldn't hear what was said due to the music, and I found myself wondering if she had slept with any of these men.

"Well?!" I called to Sal

"Well, what?"

"Have you slept with any of them?"

"That's a bit personal, Alex!" We both started laughing. "And that would be telling."

We had a couple of drinks and went for a dance. I couldn't understand what all the fuss was about, and I certainly didn't think it was worth all the money, which I then realised we hadn't paid. "Sal, who do we pay?"

"It's ok, I've already taken care of it."

"When? I didn't see you?"

"I paid over the phone on my card. It's easier that way, and anyway you don't pay tonight. You're my guest."

We carried on dancing and were approached a couple of times, but I think Sal knew I felt awkward. I don't know what she said, but the guys didn't hang around. We had another drink and found a seat.

“How did you get rid of those guys, Sal?”

“I told them we were a couple and not interested in men.” I stared back at her and we both collapsed laughing. "So, shall we go for a wander around?"

“Well, to be honest, Sal, I'm ok in here. I’m quite enjoying it."

"Oh, come on! That's what we’ve come for, so you can see what all the fuss is about!"

I nervously sipped my drink and smiled back at her. "Yes, of course, but I'm quite enjoying it in here now."

"Alex, are you getting cold feet?"

"Don’t be soft! Of course not! Come on, let's go." I quickly finished my glass of wine and followed Sal.

As we approached the first door, it was then I noticed they all had signs on them. The first one we entered was called The Sensory Room.

"We'll start you off on something quite tame," said Sal. The heady feeling the wine had given me seemed to have suddenly worn off.

Sal slowly turned the large brass door knob, and my heart began thumping yet again. There were six separate areas in this room, each containing various pieces of furniture and ‘equipment.’ On one bed lay a woman, probably mid-thirties, wearing stockings, a basque and thong, with a base colour of black and trimmed with red. The basque tied at the back with red ribbon. She lay face down on the bed and standing over her was a middle-aged man, completely naked except for a mask. He held an ostrich feather in his right hand, which he slowly ran over the woman. I covered my face as I felt I might giggle. Sal looked over at me sternly and shook her head. It was clear this place had rules, but at the same time, it didn’t.

. . .

On the next bed a naked couple were playing with food, strategically placing it on each other and then eating it off. On a third bed a man lay completely naked except for a blindfold. A woman was teasing him, giving him minimal access to her, by brushing herself against him. I didn't know what to think at this point, except I found it all a bit weird.

"We maybe ought to go, Sal."

"Why, what's wrong?"

"Nothing, I'm just not sure this is for me." I made my way back to the door we came through. I exited into the hallway and caught my breath. I had felt like I was suffocating in there.

"Are you ok?" I felt a hand on my shoulder and turned around to see a tall man stood behind me, wearing a smart suit and tie. He extended his hand out to mine. "I'm Thomas - or Tom to my friends."

His hands were strong, yet soft to touch. I was guessing he was some sort of business man due to his attire, a strong silent type, Sal would have said.

"I'm Alex..." I felt myself blushing as I said it, wondering if I should have given my real name.

"Well, Alex, would you like a drink?"

I glanced over his shoulder to see if I could spot Sal and just caught sight of her going into another room. And then I found myself saying, "Yes thank you, Tom. I'd love a dry white wine please." We made our way into the main room again. Tom ordered our drinks from the barman and said, "Let's grab a seat over here."

CHAPTER EIGHT

We sat down in a quiet corner of the room, which made it possible to have a conversation without shouting at each other.

"So, what do you think of it here, Alex?"

"Sorry, what do you mean?"

"Oh, come on, I know it's your first time," he smirked.

"Is it that obvious?"

Tom laughed. "I'm afraid so, you look a little bit lost."

"That's probably because I feel it. This was my friend's idea and I'm not sure it's for me."

"Have you seen it all?"

"No, just that one room."

"And did that put you off?"

"Well, it just felt strange and I wasn't sure it was for me."

"Maybe I should show you round...?" Tom took my hand and led me out of the room. He opened the door to The Fantasy Room and ushered me in. My first sight was a round bed in the middle of the room.

Two women were on the bed, one dressed in a leather one piece, and the other had only a thong on. There was a man sat in a chair near the bed masturbating while he watched the women. Tom looked over and asked, "Would you prefer to go upstairs?"

I looked across at him wondering what could conceivably be upstairs. He grabbed my hand again and led me into the hallway, where we made our way up the large staircase.

"Are you ready for this, Alex?" I nodded slowly, wondering what could possibly be behind the next door.

“Adagio for Strings” was playing gently in the background, and there were numerous bodies entwined on cushions on the floor. It was hard to tell what arm, leg and voice belonged to whom. There were screams, moans and groans as everyone pleasured each other. A wave of shock came over me. It was like some sort of X-rated movie you hear about.

"So, what do you think to this, Alex?" I could hear Tom’s voice in the background.

I looked back at him and smiled nervously, then spun round to head back out the door. I hurriedly made my way downstairs as he followed. Tom led me back down stairs, made his way to the bar and ordered us some more drinks. I glanced around the room but couldn't see Sal anywhere. I wondered where she was, and more importantly, who she was with. Tom nodded towards an empty table. "Come on." I followed him over and we sat in silence for a while.

"So, Alex, is this not what you were expecting?"

"Erm... well... yes and no." Tom just laughed. I looked back at him in annoyance.

"Well, it's either one or the other, Alex. I don't think it's what you were expecting."

In all honesty I didn't know what I was expecting; I

hadn't thought it through. Although it seemed like a good idea at the time, after a couple of bottles of wine, I think I had made a mistake. Just because I had experienced a new sexual encounter, it didn't mean I had to expose myself to a whole new world of intimacy. I could feel the tears welling up; in an effort to disguise my upset, I briskly blinked and casually glanced around the room.

"Look, Alex, I didn't mean to offend you. I'm just curious as to what brought you here."

"It was not what but 'who,' and the 'who' is my friend – Sal." I glanced over to Tom and threw him a sarcastic smile.

"That's better, nice to see you smile. Shall we start again?"

I glanced down at my glass and caught sight of my watch. It was 1:30am. "Jeez, I better get home."

"That's a shame, Alex... Come on, I'll take you."

"No, I'm fine, I wouldn't dream of it, and anyway you've been drinking."

Tom looked across at me and smiled. "I meant I'll book a taxi."

I glanced back at him. "Listen, that's really nice of you but, it... well, it wouldn't be right and...."

"It's ok, Alex, I'm aware that you're probably married, most people here are. I'll book you a taxi."

Tom got up from the table, took his mobile out from his pocket and left the room. I stayed seated trying to make sense of the evening and wondering what walks of life the clientele here were from. Whatever it was, they all seemed very comfortable in their skin and happy to be there, something I didn't feel.

Tom walked back in the room and beckoned me towards the

door. I got up, grabbed my bag and walked towards him. He caught my hand in his and we made our way over to the exit.

Adam was still there. "Goodnight, Mr Clark."

"Night, Adam."

A taxi was waiting for me outside. "Look, Alex, I've really enjoyed your company tonight. Maybe we could meet for a drink sometime? This is my card, give me a ring."

"Tom... I'm not sure that's a good idea."

He gently kissed my cheek and I climbed into the taxi.

It felt like I was home in no time. I didn't speak a word to the driver. I suppose I felt quite embarrassed about where he had collected me from. I arrived at my house and reached for my purse. "It's ok, Mr Clark has paid."

"But when? And how? I mean he doesn't know where I live."

"Oh no, he has an account."

"I see... ok, thank you." I left the taxi and made my way into the house.

The house was silent. James would be in bed and I'm sure the boys would still be out. I made myself a hot drink and switched the TV on for a while. After around ten minutes, I found I couldn't concentrate and actually felt quite tired, so decided to make my way up to bed. But I couldn't sleep. James was snoring away, and my mind was too preoccupied with the events of the evening. How had I let myself get involved in it all? It just wasn't me.

I must have drifted off to sleep as the next thing I heard was the boys coming in. I could hear them rustling up something in the kitchen, which was a regular occurrence in our house after a night out.

. . .

The next day I rang Sal to see how she had got on. "Yeah, it was a good night. Al, what happened to you?"

"Oh, I was just tired, I got a taxi home."

"Oh right, I thought you had hooked up with Tom."

I was surprised that Sal knew him, although I guess I shouldn't have been. "Do you want to meet for lunch tomorrow, Sal?" I was curious to know what had happened and how well she knew Tom.

"Yeah, sure, let's say one, shall we?"

"Yes, that's great, see you tomorrow."

Just then James walked into to room. "Who's that then?"

"It was Sal, just meeting up for lunch tomorrow."

"Must be nice to be able to do lunch as often as you two do." I glanced across at James and threw him a smile; he didn't even look up, his head buried in the newspaper.

The next day I met Sal for lunch at a little coffee shop in the town centre. "So, what happened with Tom then?"

"Nothing. We just chatted, had a drink and then headed home."

"Hmm, so he didn't want you to give him a slapping then?" Sal giggled as she said it.

"Hell no, what you on about?"

"Nothing... forget it."

"Sal, have you and Tom...? Well, you know what I mean."

“No, he's not on my wavelength. We don't like the same things."

"So, what is he into then?"

"Oh, you'll find out soon, when you see him again..."

I looked across at Sal. "What makes you think I'll see him again?"

"Well, when you go back!"

"And who said I was going back?"

"Oh, come on, Al, you're not giving up on it, are you? At least give it a chance." Sal got up from her chair. "Just nipping to the loo."

I stared into my coffee cup. There was something about Tom, and I suppose I should thank him for paying for the taxi. Just then I remembered the business card he had given me. I reached into my handbag, rummaging around trying to find it. Damn, I thought, it was in my other bag. I would have to look for it when I got home and give him a ring. Just to thank him, that's all.

Sal returned from the loo. "So what happened to you on Friday night, Sal?"

She casually took a sip of her coffee, looked across at me, gave a cheeky grin and replied, "Not much, really."

"So, you didn't get off with anyone?"

"Alex, it's not about 'getting off' with anyone, it's just sex. Pure sex, that's all."

"You seem so casual about it."

"That's because that's what it is, Hun, just casual sex. A bit like your Maria in Greece."

"No, it's not the same at all. I mean, it wasn't planned at all, it just happened."

"So, you don't think this Maria has done this before?"

"Well, no... at least I don't think so..."

"Alex, you have a lot to learn about life."

"What do you mean by that?"

"Nothing. Look, I've got to go. We'll catch up next week, take care, Hun." Sal leant forward, kissed me on the cheek and headed out the door. I sat for another ten minutes looking out of the window. People-watching was a favourite pastime of mine. I was wondering what tangled webs everyone else had created in their lives. I glanced at my watch and realised that I should be heading back home too.

CHAPTER NINE

I couldn't really concentrate on anything when I got home. My mind was preoccupied, thinking about Tom, wondering what his world was like, marriage, children, etc. There was no one at home, and the boys were nowhere to be seen, and judging by the pots left on the table, they had already helped themselves to some lunch. I made myself a coffee, popped a CD on and chilled out on the sofa. Then I remembered the card.

I ran upstairs to our room, searching for the bag I had used on Friday night. When I eventually found it, the card was still tucked away in the zip compartment.

I headed back down stairs with it, grabbed my mobile phone and started to dial the number. I paused halfway through. What if his wife answered? What if he didn't want to speak? Well, I was only thanking him, and if his wife answered, I just wouldn't speak.

I nervously continued to dial the rest of the number. I listened as the phone dialled out, but no one answered. Just as I was about to put the handset down, the answer phone kicked in. After a long pause, I left my message. "Oh, hi, Tom, it's Alex. Erm... well I just wanted to say thank you for Friday night, and the taxi... and well, thanks anyway... bye."

What a dreadful message, I thought, maybe I shouldn't have left one? Oh well, it was done now. For some strange reason I was trembling. I poured myself a large glass of wine and sank back into the sofa. I wished I could take back my call to Tom. What was I thinking? He probably thought I was interested in him now and I was only being courteous really.

I had almost finished my glass of wine when my mobile phone rang, I nearly jumped out of my skin. I looked at the number on the screen; it wasn't a number I recognised and there was no name attached to it. I answered anyway. "Hello."

"Hi, is that, Alex?" It was Tom; his voice was rich like dark chocolate, better than I remembered.

"Yes, it's me, did you get my message?"

"Of course, that's why I'm calling." He chuckled to himself as he said it.

"Oh, yes, well that's good then... So yeah thanks for paying for the taxi, but you didn't have to."

"Its fine, not a problem, Alex. I was hoping that you would ring. I wondered if you fancied meeting up sometime."

"Oh, I don't know really, you see I'm a bit snowed under with work and on top of that I am married."

"Well, yes, I know, Al. We discussed that on Friday."

"Oh, yes, we did." I nervously laughed down the phone.

"So how about it then? Just a friendly drink."

"Well, maybe just a quick one then."

Tom laughed softly down the phone. "How about a week on Friday then?"

"Erm, yes, a Friday's good for me, what time?"

"Shall we say eight; would you like me to send you a taxi?"

"No, it's fine I can organise my own taxi. Where do you want to meet?"

"Do you want to go back to Secret Dreams? It's probably a good place to meet."

"Erm... I, erm, well, yes, ok. Oh, but I'm not a member; Sal signed me in."

"It's ok, Alex, I can sign you in as my guest."

"Ok then, Tom, I'll see you Friday at about eight."

"Great. I look forward to it."

Tom put the phone down, and I was left stunned with myself. All the advances I had fought off from Jack and here I was meeting a man I hardly knew in a seedy club. Then again, we were only meeting for a chat and a drink, weren't we?

The weekend had passed by too quickly, as usual. In no time, it was Monday and I was back in at work. I couldn't concentrate at all and I really didn't want to be there. I didn't even want to make small talk with Susan and Lily today. I really couldn't be bothered.

When I got home, Sal popped round for a coffee. She liked to come over when she had the time, and it always seemed to put James in a good mood, so I didn't mind. He enjoyed the friendly banter he had with her, but I felt that this time she had probably come around to find out what the latest gossip was. "Well, I'm off up for a bath are you coming to scrub my back, Sal?"

"Aww, sorry, James, I need to be getting off soon, maybe next time." Sal gave James a cheeky wink as he headed out the door.

"Well, how was, Mr Grey?"

“Who? That’s not his name, and keep your voice down.”

“Oh, stop panicking! James will be in the bath by now.”

“So, what do you mean, Sal...? Mr Grey?” I glanced over at her as she threw her head back and laughed.

“Oh, Alex, you’re so naïve. I can’t believe you don’t know who he is. Let’s just say Tom is a Mr Grey wannabe.”

“I haven’t got a clue what you’re talking about but I’m pretty sure he’s just an ordinary guy.” Sal proceeded to tell me I had a lot to learn about Tom, and I didn’t realise it might be sooner than I think.

Friday came around quickly, and I was left with the problem of having nothing to wear again. The little black dress was my saviour as always. James didn't seem too bothered when I said I was going out. He had his paper and the sports channel, what more could he want.

My little black dress didn't let me down. It was like an old familiar friend and fit me like a glove. I looked through my underwear drawer for some tights to wear and came across some seamed hold up stockings that I had never worn.

I gently gathered a stocking between my fingers, placing it over my toe and slowly rolled it up my leg. The lace top sat nicely on my thigh and made me feel sexy. I finished getting ready, added a splash of perfume and headed down stairs. My taxi was booked and due any second, as I entered the living room James glanced up from the TV across at me, then did a double take and looked again. "Bloody hell, who got you ready?"

"Very funny."

"Well I don't remember you dressing like that when we last went out."

"Try casting your mind back to the last time you took me

out." You might be some time, I thought. At that point the taxi blew his horn and I headed for the door.

CHAPTER TEN

The driver didn't seem to want to chat during my journey to the club and there was an awkward silence in the car. It seemed to take forever to get there. We approached the large wrought iron gates. The driver briefly got out to do his secret handshake stuff, and as before, the gates opened.

As I got to the door, Tom was waiting outside, something I wasn't expecting. "Hi, Alex." His voice was low, sexy.

"Hi, hope I'm not late?"

"Not at all. In fact, you're five minutes early." Oh god, I hoped he didn't think I was desperate or even keen on him. "Come on, Alex. You look like you could use a drink."

We wandered through to the main room and leant against the bar waiting to be served. "Alex, you look delicious."

I giggled like some love-sick teenager. It was a long time since someone had said something like that to me, except maybe Jack once or twice. "Well, I don't know what to say. I hope that's not a leading question to take me into one of the rooms."

"It was a compliment, Alex, just a compliment."

I glanced round the room and noticed it was filled with most of the same faces that were here the last time I came, although there were some new faces to be seen. Tom eventually got served and we made our way to a table in the corner, the same we had sat at during my last visit. We chatted for a while about work and the nature of our jobs.

"So, how come you decided to give it another try here, Alex?"

I smiled back at Tom and replied, "Curiosity, I guess. It killed the cat you know." We both laughed.

"But seriously, Alex, do you want to have another look round?"

I looked back at Tom and shrugged my shoulders. He stood up and held his hand out to me. "I'll take that as a yes."

I took his hand and he led me out the room towards the staircase. "So, where does this lead?"

"Shall we say this is where I feel all the serious stuff takes place?"

I wasn't sure what Tom meant by that, but I was soon to find out.

He led me into a hallway that had another staircase and another suited guy on the door. We followed another couple up the stairs which lead to a viewing area, with seats for about six people. We sat down opposite another couple. The male was shackled to the wall wearing only a leather thong and the woman had a leather basque with stockings on. She had what I would describe as some sort of paddle in her hand and was hitting him across his already marked bottom.

I leant towards Tom and whispered, "What will his wife say when he gets home?" We both laughed.

"That might be his wife," he replied.

"I very much doubt it."

The guy let out a moan every time she hit him, and she muttered some orders to him. I turned to Tom. "What could he possibly be getting from this?"

Tom looked back at me in surprise as if I had asked him the most disgusting question ever. Then the penny dropped; Sal had asked me if Tom had wanted me to slap him. He was into this. "Can we go, Tom? I want to go."

He looked a little disappointed. "Yeah, sure..." We left the room and wandered towards the main door into the building. At the last-minute, Tom led me back into the main room. "Look, Alex, let's just have a drink."

I looked for a seat whilst Tom bought us both a drink from the bar. I leant across. "It's quiet in here now, isn't it? They must all be screwing upstairs."

Tom looked at me and laughed. "You're so wrong, Alex. It's not all about screwing." I looked back at him indignantly and asked, "So, just what is it about then?"

"Alex, I'm like him upstairs. I like that sort of thing."

"But what can you possibly get out of it? I always thought that sort of stuff was a bit freaky."

"Oh, so I'm a freak now, am I?" Tom laughed.

"No, you're not, and that's why I'm so surprised. You seem really nice and normal."

"NORMAL! You're so naive, Alex. All I ask is that you give it a try."

I looked back at him and laughed out loud. "You've got to be kidding me! My idea of a night out is not beating someone up."

Tom went on to explain to me about how it wasn't like that, and when I said I wouldn't want to be observed, he told me we could hire a private room. I left the house that night with my head spinning, wondering what it was all about, and how that could turn anyone on.

Over the next few days I spent my spare time looking up 'Sadomasochism' and 'Dominatrix' on the internet. I couldn't believe how popular it was and how many people out there were into it. I even broached the subject with Lily and Susan, making out I had read an article in the paper about an increase in the sale of sex toys.

"Yes, I heard that too," Lily replied. "It's due to the massive sale of that book."

"What book, Lily?" With that Susan stopped typing and coasted towards me on her chair.

"Oh, you know, the one with Mr Grey."

Hmm, Mr Grey again, I thought... "Actually, no I don't know, I've not read it."

"You're joking!" Lily said. "Everyone has read it!"

"Well, not me, so what's all the fuss about?"

Susan took it up from there. "Well, he's a bit of a control freak, likes to be in charge."

"Who? And in charge of what?"

"Oh, you have to read the book, I'll lend you it."

. . .

I began to think I had been living in a bubble after my long chat with Lily and Susan, some of the things they were coming out with. I decided to get in touch with Sal and see if she was free to meet up for a few drinks later. As always, she was happy to. She was always free for a drink. I met her at our usual wine bar that evening.

"So, what's wrong, Alex?"

"Nothing's wrong. Why do you always assume there is something wrong?"

"Oh, I don't know. After your latest antics, I don't know what to expect."

"Well, sorry to disappoint you, Sal, but there is nothing wrong."

"Well, that's good then, so what have you been up to? Have you seen anything of Tom?"

I didn't need to say anything. She could read me like a book and she knew straight away that I had seen him. She was so clued up on him, I had to ask, "Have you been with him, Sal?"

"Hell no, Al, he's not my type."

"Well, you seem to know a lot about him."

"I've known him for some time now."

She went on to tell me all about Tom and about how she wasn't into the same things as him and what he liked in bed. If Sal wasn't into it, I was certain that I wouldn't be. It was then I admitted to her, "I'm struggling to understand what it's all about. I've been on the internet this week checking out the various sites. There's loads at it." At this point, Sal nearly fell off her chair in fits of laughter. I looked at her bemused.

"Oh, I'm sorry, Alex. I just can't imagine you doing that."

"Well, I haven't... I mean won't... Well I wouldn't, would I?"

She looked up from her drink and said, "Well, do you know, I don't know if you would or not." I took another sip from my glass, and quickly changed the subject because, in all honesty, neither did I.

CHAPTER ELEVEN

The next day while at work I received an unexpected text from Tom.

Do you fancy going out tonight?

I thought for a minute before replying.

Do you mean somewhere normal?

A few minutes went by before he replied.

LOL, yes somewhere NORMAL!

I paused before sending my response.

Yes, ok what time?

We arranged to meet in a small bar in the old town. I got

there just after eight. Tom was already waiting for me. There was something different about him tonight. He was dressed casually in an open necked polo shirt and jeans, and I was used to seeing him in suits. He looked towards me from the bar and awkwardly ran his fingers through his dark brown hair as I approached him. The familiar scent of his aftershave aroused my senses. He leant towards me, kissed me on the cheek and whispered hello in my ear, "As usual, you look lovely."

"Thank you." I smiled. It was a warm summer evening and I had worn an ocean blue dress, which clung to every inch of me. We briefly chatted about work and what we had been up to, before getting onto the subject that was the elephant in the room.

"So, have you thought anymore about things then?"

I looked into his smouldering brown eyes and replied. "Actually, yes, I've been looking it up on the internet."

He laughed. "My god, Alex, you've probably put yourself off all together!"

"Well, I have to say there is a lot of it out there."

Tom proceeded to explain to me why he was the way he was and what he got out of it. I still didn't understand it, but I was beginning to understand him and realised that there was a definite attraction between us. We stayed in the wine bar all night and the time went by so quickly. It was after midnight as I rose from my seat and explained that I would have to go.

"Ok, Cinders, I understand." I turned back to look at him and we both laughed. Tom walked me towards the taxi queue, but as we were approaching it, he suddenly pulled me into a doorway, kissed me and then kissed me again harder, pressing his whole body against mine.

I felt like I couldn't breathe. I could feel his hard cock against me and I wanted him, no kinky stuff – just him. His tongue seemed to be exploring every part of my mouth. I didn't want him to stop but if I didn't pull away it may result in sex in a doorway. We paused to catch our breath. "I really must go."

"Ok listen, Al. I have a business meeting in a couple of weeks in Halifax, and I'm booking a hotel for the night. I want you to come with me."

I stared back at Tom, a thousand thoughts running through my head. *Could I get the time off? What would I tell James? And if I did go what should I expect?* "I don't know, I'll have to think about it."

"OK, just let me know."

Just then a taxi pulled up at the taxi rank. "Look, there's a taxi... I better go."

He pulled me towards him kissing me softly and whispered in my ear, "Night. Call me."

"Night, Tom, I will." I ran across to the car and waved to him as the taxi drove past.

During the week that followed I was busy with work, which was just as well as James was working late most nights, and it meant that I didn't have to face him too much.

Although nothing had happened between Tom and me, except for that kiss, I knew I wanted it to. It was only a couple of days after that night that I received a text from Tom.

Have you decided yet? X

I couldn't reply and say I hadn't thought about it; I had thought of nothing else. I thought I could maybe tell James I was visiting an old friend, although I may struggle convincing him with it being the middle of the week. I texted Tom back:

I'll let you know at the end of the week x

I told James later that week that my friend had called, that she was having a bad time and needed a shoulder. He seemed convinced and not too concerned that I was staying over. I used the same excuse with work to avoid any confusion and used some of the flexi time I was owed.

I texted Tom later that week to find out what the arrangements were. We agreed to meet at a hotel, late afternoon on the Wednesday. The time flew by, and before I knew it, it was Tuesday and I was packing an overnight bag. I didn't mention it to Sal; I couldn't face all the questions.

The next day I woke up early, tidied round and made sure there were some meals prepared for James and the boys, as I knew if I didn't the takeaway would benefit from them. Time flew by and it was soon mid-day. I had a quick shower, dried my hair and headed out to the car. It was only an hour's drive away and the traffic was pretty quiet, so I was there in no time.

I pulled up to the hotel, which turned out to be a nice four star, quite plush and comfortable looking. I made my way to the main lounge where I had arranged to meet Tom and to my surprise he was there already. He got up from the leather couch to greet me, doing that thing with his hair that always gave me a warm feeling inside. He kissed me on my cheek, and his scent seemed to cast a spell on me. I wanted to hold on to him tightly but managed to hold back.

"Have you been here long?"

"Not really, I managed to get off a bit earlier. Did you have a good trip?"

"Yeah, it was fine."

We made small talk for a while and shared a bottle of good quality wine that was full of body, flavour and a high percentage of alcohol. Tom soon asked if I would like to get settled into the room. My stomach did a somersault and I nervously agreed. This was so alien to me — a secret rendezvous in a hotel – I couldn't get my head round it.

"You ok?" Tom asked. He must have noticed I was deep in thought.

"Yes, I'm fine. Why?"

"You just seem a little distant."

I glanced up at him and smiled as we entered the lift to go up to the room. I let my gaze fall and concentrated on the doors in front of me but could feel his eyes burning into me. I looked across at him, smiling nervously. What was I thinking? I hardly knew this man, and here I was about to share a hotel room with him far from home, not knowing what to expect. I turned and smiled at him again, and I knew that, however wrong it was, when I looked at his dark mahogany hair and chocolate brown eyes with little flecks of hazel, I knew I wanted him. And that's all that mattered right now.

We finally reached our floor and stepped out of the lift, walked a short distance along the corridor and came to a stop outside room 203. We were here. Tom slipped the card into the door and held it open as I stepped inside. He followed, and the door closed softly behind us. I turned back to face him, and he kissed me, the same way he did before in the doorway. I could hardly breathe as he pushed me against the wall, holding my arms up, kissing my neck, moving down towards my breasts, biting at my clothes.

His lips met mine again. I could feel his cock pushing against me through his trousers. I felt so wet and I just wanted him inside me. I broke away from his grasp and tried to undo his belt, but I was shaking so much, it took a while. The frustration was beginning to build up. I undid the zip on his trousers, slipped my hand into his boxers, and then I felt it. So firm and hard in my hand, and I wanted him now.

Tom hitched my skirt up past my waist, revealing my stocking tops. His hand searched for the naked flesh of my thigh above my stocking, and he moaned out loud when he found it. His hand moved between my legs and pulled my knickers to the side, pushing his finger inside of me. There was no further need for foreplay; I was so wet, and I wanted him now.

"Now please, now!" I cried out. I helped Tom remove my panties, and he picked me up. I wrapped my legs around him and quickly slid onto his cock. I moaned with delight. I could feel him deep inside me.

"Oh God, I'm coming... No, not yet... Oh please, not yet." And with that I let out a loud moan of delight.

Tom carried me to the bed, still hard inside me. He lay me down and began to push into me, slowly at first, my juices squeezing out with every move. He thrust harder, and I could feel him deep inside me. Suddenly, he stopped and looked down at me. "Turn around."

"Why?" I asked.

"Just turn around, I want to see your arse." *Hmm*, I thought, *I know someone else who has a fascination with my arse.*

I let him pull away and quickly turned over. I pulled back onto my knees again, and he was soon inside me again.

God I was so hungry for him, and I didn't want it to end. Without warning, he slapped my arse and squeezed it straight after.

"Hey, whoa, what do you think you're doing?"

"Just go with it," Tom said. "I promise I won't hurt you. It's just fun. I would never hurt you."

I was slightly stunned, and my second orgasm looked unlikely now. I tried to get back into the swing of it but couldn't refocus my mind. Tom sensed how I was feeling, so a few minutes later he came, and we just lay together. I couldn't understand why he had done that and spoilt the moment.

"What are you thinking?" Tom asked.

"Nothing," I lied.

"I think I can guess," he replied.

I sat up and looked at him. "Well, what was all that about?"

"Look, Alex, it was no big deal. I was just playing around. I didn't hurt you, did I?"

"Well, no, you didn't, but I was a bit shocked."

Tom began to laugh, whilst I stared indignantly back at him. "The look on your face was priceless."

"Well, I'm glad you think so… I nearly walked out."

Tom began laughing heartily, and it was no good. I couldn't control it any longer and fell back onto the bed laughing with him. He wrapped his arms around me and stroked my hair. I must have fallen asleep, and when I woke up, I could hear him in the shower. I snuggled further under the duvet as he wandered back through in a fluffy white towel.

"Hi, are you hungry? I thought we could go down for dinner."

"Yes, that sounds good. I'll go for a shower."

I grabbed my overnight bag that I hadn't even had chance to unpack and made my way into the bathroom. I stepped into the cubicle and turned the shower on, reaching for the complimentary shower gel and slowly lathering my body with the suds. With the sound of the shower, I was unable to hear Tom enter the room and I jumped as he entered the shower. I spun round to face him.

"Turn back around," he whispered in my ear.

I turned around to face the wall, his strong hands sliding around the curves of my body. He gently moved his hands down and between my thighs, and I ached for him to take me now. The water kissed my skin as it left the shower, and Tom gently coaxed me round to face him, pressing me up against the cold wall of tiles. Our lips met, and as the water caressed my skin once more, I felt the surge of his kiss drive through my body, leaving a tingling under my skin.

Both his hands searched for my rear, squeezing it with force. He lifted me up and I wrapped my legs around his hips. He gently slid into me as I began to pant. He let out a groan with every thrust. I felt him deeper and deeper inside me. He gently cupped my breasts and I moaned at the feel of his warm hands.

My nipples stood hard and erect as he moved down towards them, covering them with his lips. I ran my fingers through his dark wet hair, pulling it as he began to kiss me, his lips soft as silk, wet and warm. The rush suddenly soared through my body, and I let out a cry as I climaxed.

Tom was still hard and pushing inside me, till finally his body tensed and his time arrived. We both relaxed, and he lowered me back to the ground. We began to shower together, but this time actually showering.

Afterwards, I slipped into a fitted black dress, which I felt was appropriate for dinner, and a pair of seamed stockings with some red lace French knickers, which I felt was appropriate for dessert.

After dinner we sat in the lounge area and chatted about several things, but I couldn't resist getting back onto the subject of fetishes.

"The way you talk about this, Alex, you would think I was the only person into this."

"No, you've got me all wrong. I don't think that at all. It's just that it's all new to me."

I realised Tom couldn't understand why I found it all a little weird, but I had been in an almost missionary marriage for the past twenty odd years, and that's all I had known. Well, except for my experience with Maria.

"You're drifting off again, Alex."

"No, I'm not, I'm fine. Look, let's just relax and enjoy tonight."

"That sounds good to me."

We both began chatting again, putting the world to rights and people watching. We didn't stop talking and laughing all night, and I had to admit I felt comfortable with Tom.

The evening went by quickly and we were soon making our way back towards the lift to go up to our room. I stepped inside, and Tom followed, gently squeezing my arse with his strong hands. The door closed slowly behind us and as it did Tom said, "I want to fuck you in here now, Alex."

The wine had made me heady and relaxed. I giggled and leaned back against wall of the lift. Tom reached for my hemline and yanked my skirt up, slid his fingers around both sides of my knickers and pulled them down. I could feel his hot breath against my ear lobe. I kissed him hard and then drew away panting.

"But what if we stop and someone gets in?"

"We won't, and they won't," Tom replied and he pressed another button on the lift. My hand reached for his cock again, and I slowly rubbed it against his trousers. I could feel it erect and bulging against the fabric, waiting for me. We both fumbled to get his trousers undone and then there it was, standing proud. As he slid it inside me, I let out a long moan.

"Jeez, Alex." Tom pushed harder and faster into me. I felt the rush and screamed out. It was over quickly, and we soon came to. The lift began to slow down as we approached a floor, and we only just managed to straighten ourselves up as the door opened. I glanced to the side of the lift to see we were on the twelfth floor and needed to go back down ten floors.

A couple entered the lift, and they looked like they hadn't had the best of nights. Tom had managed to press floor two, and we made our way back down.

It seemed to take forever, but we finally reached our floor. We both hurried out of the lift, laughing uncontrollably at our adventure. Back in the room, Tom asked, "Do you fancy a drink, Alex?"

"No, I'm fine thank you."

"Would you like a coffee then?"

I settled for a coffee. We both lay on the bed chatting and

laughed about the lift. "So, have you done that before, Tom?" I turned around and looked at him.

"No never."

I couldn't believe it; this man of the world had experienced something new with me.

I lay my head against his chest. He smelt good enough to eat and I think that's what he wanted. He wrapped his fingers around my long auburn hair, pulled on it and guided my head towards his erection. My lips stretched around him, slowly moving down his penis, and I could feel it pulsating as I took it all. Gently moving up and down, curling my tongue as I came up, I felt him shudder as it sent shivers down his spine. He pushed my head down hard all the way and moaned again. I grabbed his balls in my hand, rolling them between my fingers. He cried out, and I felt his warm semen hit the back of my throat. I relaxed and lay my head against his leg.

"That was amazing," he said. I looked up at him and smiled.

CHAPTER TWELVE

Our time away ended quickly, and before I knew it, we were heading our separate ways. I was pleased to have my memories of the weekend with Tom, and I couldn't quite believe it had all happened. It all seemed a bit like a dream. I couldn't describe the feelings I had about my weekend. All I know is the little devil in me had appeared and I liked it.

When I got home, James was relaxing in the living room. "Oh, you're back early. I wasn't expecting you till this evening. How is she then?"

"Who?"

"Your friend. Is she ok?"

"Oh, Jen, yeah, she's not too bad. Just going through a bad time with her husband. He's left her."

I glanced across at James, who was glued to the TV screen, not even looking up as he replied. "Oh, that's too bad."

. . .

In the weeks that followed, it wasn't that difficult to get out of the house to meet Tom. The boys were always out at rehearsals with a new band they had formed. I made an excuse to James that I was having to attend regular update meetings regarding work, and he seemed alright with that. To be honest, he was always so wrapped up in his own work that he didn't seem to notice that much at all.

I was managing to meet Tom probably every three weeks. I felt like I was under a spell – his spell – one I couldn't escape from, but more importantly, one I didn't want to escape from. It was a spell that lead to symptoms of lust and attraction. I guess it was similar to a trap; once you're in, you can't get out.

I had not seen Sal for a while too. She used to do that though, drift off now and again. I had no doubt she would be wrapped up with one of her male friends, and knowing what I know now, probably literally.

I began to think about how our lives had changed recently and realised we hadn't had Jack and Sarah round for a while. Everyone seemed too preoccupied with their own lives. I guess life is like that sometimes. You drift away from your regular friends and move in different circles for a while.

That Friday, Sarah rang out of the blue and asked if she and Jack could come around on Saturday night. Of course, I said yes, even though I didn't fancy fighting off Jack's advances again. Sarah sounded like she needed a break though, and I couldn't let her down.

I mentioned it to James when he got in from work. He didn't seem too bothered either way.

. . .

Sarah and Jack arrived around 7:30pm, but they didn't seem to be themselves. Well, actually Jack was, but Sarah seemed quiet and uneasy. I was busy preparing the usual snacks in the kitchen when she came through to join me.

"So, how are you, Sarah? I feel like we haven't seen you for ages."

"That's because we haven't been for ages." The tone in her voice was different. I glanced up at her and could tell there was something wrong. "We haven't been out since we last came here. Well, should I say *I* haven't."

She seemed on edge and angry, and I didn't really know what to say. I just looked at her openly, hoping that she would tell me what was wrong. "You see, I think Jack is..."

With that, the door from the hallway opened and in walked Jack. "So, how are my favourite girls? And what have you been up to, Alex?" He threw me a cheeky grin and winked at me. I wanted to tell him to get out, so Sarah could tell me what I think I already knew, but I didn't want him to think we were talking about him, so I humoured him.

"I'm good thanks, Jack, and you?"

He leant against the work surface next to Sarah and casually put his arm around her shoulder. "Yeah, we're good, aren't we, Hun?"

I could see Sarah just wanted to get as far away from him as possible, so I asked her to take some of the food into the lounge. As she left, Jack made his way over to me, invading my personal space as usual.

"So, how's my frigid little friend then?"

I looked up and gave him the best smile I could manage, if only you knew I thought. "You're so funny, Jack."

"Well, yeah, I like to think so. When are you going to give in, Alex? You know it's only a matter of time..."

That will never happen, I thought. While he was a good friend and attractive, he was still a lady's man and one I wouldn't want to get involved with.

Just then Sarah came back in the room. Jack poured himself another drink and headed back into the room. "Well, I'll leave you ladies to it."

I looked over at Sarah who was staring into her drink. "Sorry, what were you saying, Sarah?"

"It's Jack, Alex. He's having an affair."

This was no surprise to me. I had always known that he was messing around. it was so obvious. Heaven knows he had tried it often enough with me.

I looked up at Sarah. "What! Are you sure?" I had to at least sound surprised.

"Yes, I'm sure. He's coming home later and staying overnight sometimes. He says its work, but I know it's not. I can tell. He's so different. We don't have sex anymore. I can't even remember the last time."

As Sarah continued to tell me about her suspicions about Jack, I began to think about what I was doing to James. It was as bad if not worse than what Jack was doing to Sarah. The rest of the night seemed strained. Sarah was clearly upset, and Jack (as usual) didn't seem to care. She would be better off without him. I'm not sure she would agree though.

I constantly found myself wishing my life away, counting the days till I would be meeting with Tom again. When the time finally came, I couldn't wait to get there.

I had had a rough couple of weeks, and with trying to

console Sarah too, I needed some me time, and Tom was the perfect person to share it with.

He was waiting for me in the foyer of the hotel as usual and had ordered my drink ready for me.

"Hi, do you mind if we take these upstairs, Tom?"

He looked back at me and smiled. "No problem."

We made our way into the lift with another couple and got out on our usual floor. We somehow always managed to have the same room. I imagined Tom must have asked for it specifically.

He swiped the hotel key card into the slot, opened the door and stepped aside to let me into the room first. I walked in, and Tom followed, his hand caressing my rear as he did so. "I've missed you, Alex."

"Yes, I've missed you too." I turned round to face him and he moved forward to kiss me. I placed two fingers on his lips and said, "No, not this time. We do it my way this time." Tom went to speak and this time I held my finger to my own lips. "Shhhhh."

I asked him to sit in a chair in the corner of the room. I looked for a suitable track to play from my phone, placed it on the bedside table, and positioned myself ready.

I was wearing a black skirt and white blouse. I slowly started to undo the blouse, slipping my fingers in between the soft material as I undid each button. Before I removed it, I turned my back on Tom, watching him via the mirror hanging opposite him on the wall. I lowered the blouse off my shoulders, and it slid gently to the floor. I reached behind me to find the zip of my skirt, undid the button, then moved my hands to my hips, gently swaying them from side to side in time with the music.

I noticed Tom was starting to shuffle in his seat, his hand holding the swelling in his trousers. I undid the zip and peeled the skirt off me, exposing my black stockings. I slowly turned around to face Tom, who reached out to touch me as I walked towards him.

"No! Sit on your hands."

"Sorry, what did you say?" Tom replied.

"I said sit on your hands. You can't touch me until I say."

Tom eased his hands under his thighs. I smiled to myself; I had begun to like this authority. I moved closer to him and straddled his legs, lowering myself onto his knee. He freed one of his hands and touched my leg.

"No," I said. I grabbed his wrist and moved his hand away. "You're not listening to me. No touching."

"But I need you, Alex," he whispered.

"Not till I say." I moved away from Tom and turned my back on him again.

I slipped my fingers into the waist of my black pants, teasing him, slowly sliding my fingers up and down the edges. I started to remove them, rolling them down my legs. Tom wanted me so bad now and I was loving it. I stepped out of my pants and turned once again to face him. I pushed the straps of my black opaque bra down over my shoulders and unhooked the back, as my bra fell to the floor Tom moved towards me. Now just wearing my stockings and stilettos I pushed him back into the chair. "You must wait."

"I can't, Alex, I want you now," he murmured.

I placed my hands on his shoulders, moving myself towards him, my breasts almost touching his lips. His tongue was searching for my nipples, but I moved back quickly and smiled down at him. I lowered myself to my knees in front of him and slowly undid the zip on his trousers. By now he was practically drooling. I held his cock in my hand, so hard and ready for me, as I was for him. I stood back up, stepping backwards till I felt the bed behind me.

Laying on my side on the bed, I looked over to Tom.

"What now, Alex?"

I slowly ran my hand from my knee along my leg till my fingers felt the warm flesh at the top of my stocking. Just as I began exploring my aching body, Tom said, "Al, I need you now."

"No, now you undress for me, Tom." He quickly began to take his clothes off. "No, I mean slowly, like I did."

"Aww, come on, Alex."

I began to laugh. Tom had undressed in no time and his lips were soon touching mine.

Every inch of my body tingled in anticipation of what was coming. I felt intoxicated by the familiar smell of his aftershave and I could feel his hands slowly moving their way around my body, heightening my already charged senses. His fingers caressed me like they had known me forever, knowing just where to go and just what to do. Every nerve in me was aroused and I wanted him inside me.

His lips moved down, and he gently parted my legs, the ache in me was like never before. As his lips found me, I reached for the headboard and begged him not to stop.

And he didn't. He explored me like every inch of my body had an unknown secret to him waiting to be found. I could feel he was ready and waiting for me, and I was ready for him.

"Now, Tom, please now."

He looked up at me and smiled. "I should make you wait."

I edged towards him as he rolled over and made my way up towards his face, gently exploring his body with my lips, brushing them against his strong thighs. He stood erect, teasing me. I needed him, and I had waited so long.

I pressed myself against him and eased my way up his torso until our lips met. As I sat astride him, he gently slipped inside me and I groaned with pleasure. I moved back and forth, feeling him inside me, moving faster and pushing him deeper and deeper.

I could feel the rush that was coming, building up like an explosion inside me. My body tensed like a spasm as I came, and Tom groaned as he reached his climax.

He fell back onto the bed next to me, and I lay my head on his chest, watching him breathing, wondering how I had come to be here. All these secret meetings and wild sex, James would be so shocked, and Jack would never believe it. Come to think of it neither could I.

CHAPTER THIRTEEN

The next day we woke early and headed down to the restaurant within the hotel to eat breakfast. Tom announced that he had taken the day off and asked if I would like a browse round the shops. That was something that I wasn't used to. James would rather run a mile than go shopping with me.

The morning seemed to fly by. We hadn't been in many shops but had walked a lot and I was beginning to feel the strain in my heels.

"Shall we break for lunch?" Tom asked

"I would love to," I sighed. I can't deny I was relieved and definitely ready for something to eat. We found a nice cosy café and settled down for lunch. I just had a jacket potato with a cheese filling, whilst Tom had some sort of baguette with chips. I found myself watching him as he ate, thinking about how much he turned me on. I couldn't remember ever feeling that way about James, ever.

"You're drifting again, Alex."

I looked across at him and smiled, thinking, *No, I'm not I'm right here.*

After we finished eating and were having our coffee, Tom looked up at me and said, "Alex, there's somewhere I want to show you."

I looked across at Tom with curiosity. "And where would that be?"

"Well, it would be easier just to take you there."

Surely, it couldn't be as shocking as Secret Dreams, I thought and agreed to go, and after all, I trusted him now.

We made our way back to the hotel to collect Tom's car. We had been travelling a few minutes when I turned and asked, "Where is this place?"

"It's about five miles from here, not too far."

After another ten minutes or so, we pulled into a small street, got out of the car, and stepped into a reasonably small shop.

It was like a wonderland, and as I entered, I thought I had travelled back in time. Hung on the walls were various costumes and masks from sometime in the 17th Century. Tom was obviously a regular customer here as he was given a warm and friendly welcome by the man behind the counter.

"Good afternoon, Mr Clark. How are you?"

Tom continued to make small talk with the shopkeeper for a short while.

"Is it ok if we go through to the back and have a look?"

"Certainly, Mr Clark, no problem."

. . .

From the conversation, I established that this was a hire shop and the costumes ranged from the 15th Century upwards. When we went through to the back, I was amazed at what I saw. The shop was a lot larger than I had first thought, with a full wall of masquerade masks and hundreds of costumes. Tom asked if I would like to try some things on, and I had to be honest; I couldn't wait. The outfits were beautiful.

I wandered around looking at all the different items on offer as Tom put some things together for me to try. He came over with a full outfit, consisting of a basque, a beautiful full-length dress, a mask and a wig. I'd be left completely in disguise, which I think was his aim. I made my way into the changing room with my costume in hand, eager to try it on.

After some time struggling with the basque and the corset part of the dress, I emerged from behind the curtain to model my outfit to Tom, complete with wig and mask.

"Wow! I'd like to fuck you right now," Tom said out loud. I looked in the mirror and couldn't believe the transformation. I looked like someone else, and I felt different too.

Tom had chosen a costume whilst I was changing and went to try it on. When he emerged from the changing room, he looked totally different. In fact, if I didn't already know it was him, I wouldn't have recognised him at all.

I changed back into my clothes and when I came out Tom was at the counter.

"Did you feel comfortable in that, Alex?"

"Yes, I did actually."

"Great, we will take both costumes then please." I looked across at Tom and wondered what he could be playing at.

"Would Madam like any makeup?" The shop assistant asked.

"No, thank you, I have my own."

Tom then stepped in and asked if he could sort out the

makeup we would require. I looked across at him, and he smiled back at me, throwing me a cheeky wink.

After he had handed over copious amounts of cash, we left the shop. It was raining, so we hurried back to the car.

"So, tell me why you have just bought those costumes..."

"I didn't buy them, Alex, I hired them."

"Jeez, I hope you get something back when you return them!"

"Of course you do. I'm surprised you haven't asked why I've hired them."

"Well, I assume you want us to dress up?"

"Haha, well, yes. We are going to dress up; we're going to a masquerade ball tonight."

I glanced across at Tom. "A masquerade ball?!" I didn't know what to think, although inside I was a little excited at the thought of dressing up again later.

When we arrived back at the hotel, we headed straight up to the room and showered. Tom suggested we order room service and then get ready. The time seemed to fly by, and before I knew it, we were getting into our costumes. I tried asking Tom about the evening ahead, but he wasn't giving much away.

Tom had found a site on the internet that had instructions on how to apply the makeup for a masquerade ball. It took me a good hour to get ready with the complexity of the makeup and the costume, and a good half bottle of wine for Dutch courage, but I have to say, I didn't recognise myself. It felt a bit strange in some respects but also exciting at the same time.

My mask was only an eye mask, but with the white makeup on, I was definitely unrecognisable. Tom came through from the bathroom all dressed and ready to go. I didn't know him at all. He could have been anybody. He had a full suit on, a long wig and full mask. I giggled nervously at him. He took my arm and said,

"The taxi will be here shortly, shall we go?"

We arrived at a large house somewhere in the country. It reminded me of Secret Dreams, except everyone was in costume – even the doorman. We stepped through the large wooden doors and were shown into a large ballroom. *This was the business to be in,* I thought. It was like we had stepped back in time.

Tom had obviously been before. He knew the routine and guided me through the ballroom. Couples were dancing and not to anything you would hear in the charts. Beethoven's fifth symphony drifted through the air, and it all seemed strangely weird but exciting as well.

Tom didn't speak a word to me. He just gestured to where he wanted me to go with a nod of his head or a motion of his hand. He led me through a door at the back of the room, which in turn lead to a staircase. We made our way up to the first floor and entered a room which had around ten people in.

The room was fitted out with period furniture and a rich red carpet covered the floor. The guests that were present had obviously attended before as they were comfortable in their surroundings, unlike me.

Tom finally spoke for the first time. "I'm just going to the bathroom. I'll be back shortly."

"But, Tom..."

"Shush, you'll be fine."

And with that, Tom disappeared through the door. I didn't know whether to leave the room and wait for him on the landing or just wait and watch.

Just at that moment, someone stopped in front of me and in a sultry whispered tone said, "Hello, I'm Anton."

I looked up to see a man wearing a white mask and a wig that looked very similar to Tom's.

"Is that your real name?" I asked.

"Of course. Well, it's Antonio, and you are?"

I struggled to think of a name. "Erm, Susan."

Antonio laughed and threw his head back. "Could you not think of a better name than that?"

I was pleased he couldn't see my face as I scowled back at him, and I don't think Susan at work would have been too pleased about him slating her name. In spite of this, I couldn't help feeling attracted to him. His strong accent was so sexy; I was mesmerised by him. I wished I could see more of his face. I could just about make out that his eyes were a dark brown, almost black, and I imagined he was Italian by the accent, although he was probably English. Whichever it was, he turned me on. He smelt familiar, although I knew I had never met him before. I suddenly remembered where I had smelt it – it was an aftershave Jack usually wore.

I was leant against some sort of banister that was attached to the wall at certain points of the room. Antonio leaned towards me and whispered, "Turn around."

Shaking but without question. I turned around, tightly

gripping the banister. I felt his strong, firm hand pulling my long gown up, my pants were so wet with excitement and I could hardly breathe. His hand wandered until he finally found the top of my stocking. His hot breath laid against my neck as he moaned. I wanted to turn and kiss him, but I couldn't. I knew that was not allowed.

His hand slowly moved up the side of my leg, brushing my stockings, then slipped between my thighs. I moaned with pleasure and yearned for more. His finger slid underneath my pants and into me, gently pushing. I let out a cry.

I hadn't given a thought to my surroundings, or the fact that I was sharing the room with several other people. He continued to fuck me with his fingers, moving faster until I oozed with pleasure. It was only then that I opened my eyes, and I noticed I was facing a mirror.

As I stared into it, I saw Tom in the reflection, staring back at me. I tried to turn around, but Antonio was having none of it. "I haven't finished," he said, grabbing my hands and holding them against the banister. "I need to fuck you, I mean really fuck you." I glanced again in the mirror and noticed that Tom was still watching. I just wished I could see his face.

Antonio continued to fuck me hard, pushing me forward with such force. My hands clenched tightly around the bannister as my body stiffened with pleasure. A surge rushed through me. I was there, and he knew it. Suddenly he lent forward, re-arranged my dress and whispered into my ear, "Thank you," before disappearing back into the crowd.

CHAPTER FOURTEEN

I looked across at Tom, wondering what he would be thinking, as he made his way over to me.

"I need to fuck you right now."

He turned me round, hurriedly lifted my dress up, pulled my pants down and slid inside me. I was still so wet from Antonio that he went in with ease, and it felt so good to have Tom inside me.

This time I was more aware of the surroundings and the amount of people watching, but in a strange sort of way, it was turning me on more. He lifted me up so my legs wrapped around him, my body jolting as Tom was fucking me so hard. His strong hands held the cheeks of my arse, squeezing them tight. I didn't think I could come again, but I was wrong. I did and then so did he.

As I was recovering from this second surge of pleasure, Tom let me down, straightened my dress and suggested we move on to another room.

We moved up to the second floor of the building, into a room that appeared to be something that Tom may be into. In the far corner of the room, a man was secured in some stocks and naked from the waist down. His mistress held a leather whip in her hand and was whipping him hard whilst he screamed with delight.

Tom grabbed my hand and led me to one of the beds. As we made our way over, we passed an array of props, and he paused to grab a riding crop.

When we reached the bed, Tom lay down and asked me to undo his trousers. It's just as well he couldn't see the expression on my face. I had enjoyed myself so much so far, I felt it was the least I could do. I undid his belt and button, and gently slid them down.

"Don't be so soft, Alex, use some force."

As I pulled his trousers off, he rolled over onto the bed, pushing his arse towards me. He handed me the riding crop. "You know what to do with it." I reluctantly flicked it against his arse. "Come on, Al, do it like you mean it."

With that I pulled back and whipped his arse so hard, he screamed out. I quickly leaned over him and whispered in his ear, "Are you alright?"

"Never been better," he replied. "Now, do it again."

I pulled back again and whacked him as hard as I could. He let out a cry. I was really getting into this now and enjoying the feeling of control. I asked if I could blindfold him.

"Anything you say, Mistress."

I walked over to the props and grabbed both a black silk blindfold and a paddle. I wrapped the blindfold around his head, over his eyes, and tied it on tight. He knelt with his knees on the floor, bending over and letting his upper body lay on the bed. I smacked his already sore arse with the paddle. I couldn't believe how turned on I had become. I was aching for him to fuck me there and then. I slapped his bare arse with my hand as I leaned over him.

"I need you now," I whispered in his ear. He looked back at me with that knowing look in his eyes. "I want you now, Tom."

He rolled over on the bed as I hitched my long gown up and removed my panties. As I straddled him, my gown slid further up my thighs, revealing my stocking tops in the process.

"Oh, Alex!" Tom cried with passion in his voice.

I slid straight on to his ravenous cock, so hard and wanting, my pussy throbbing, letting him know I wanted him just as bad. I fucked him with an eagerness that made it seem like we had never had sex before and would never again. I pushed down hard against him, feeling him move deeper inside me, and I could feel myself beginning to come. That familiar tingling feeling starting from my toes and working its way up my body.

"Oh. Oh." I pushed down harder and faster. "Oh my God, I'm coming!"

The rush filled me like nothing before, and I physically ached afterwards. Tom relaxed back on the bed, and as we lay there, I realised I loved the costumes, but I wasn't that keen on the masks. I liked to see his face and I longed to kiss him.

We gathered ourselves together and made our way to a bar in

another room. It was overflowing with people and the heat was intense. It took some time before we eventually got served, and Tom said he needed to go to the toilet again. I had noticed a side door with a patio area as we had entered the room and suggested that I would wait for him outside to get some air.

There was a decking area that led to a private garden, and I leant against the handrail and waited for Tom. As I did, a woman approached me.

"Excuse me, darling, do you have a light?"

"No, I'm sorry, I don't smoke."

"Never mind, I should give it up anyway." She carefully placed the cigarette back into the packet and leant against the handrail next to me.

"Beautiful night, isn't it?"

"Yes, yes, it is," I replied.

"You're new here, aren't you?"

I looked over towards this stranger I had just met and wondered how she could possibly know that with all this makeup and a mask on.

The pause that became my reply must have answered her question and she laughed. "Don't worry, darling. I have a sense for these things."

She began to tell me how she was introduced to these clubs, what she liked and what she didn't. I was curious about what she was into, so I asked her about her different fetishes.

"My darling, fetish is not all about sex. It's about control. It's about telling the person if you want sex and how you want it. It's about whether they go on the top or the bottom, and you decide."

I was fascinated by this woman. She was certainly a woman of the world. She continued, "Another thing, darling,

I never go down on a man unless he's showered, squeaky clean and waxed."

I listened with intrigue and thought how it was a good job I was wearing a mask, so she couldn't see the expressions on my face and the enormity of my eyes widening. I desperately wanted to see this woman without the mask, just to see what sort of woman did this sort of thing on a regular basis.

Just then, out of the darkness, a man appeared by her side and whispered something in her ear, to which she replied, "My darling, I don't spit, I swallow, and believe me you couldn't handle me."

I almost choked on my drink; I couldn't believe she had just said that. Tom suddenly reappeared and our conversation ended.

"Come on, we're leaving," he said as he grabbed my hand.

I quickly called back to the mystery woman, "Nice to have met you."

"Yes, you too, darling. Maybe I will see you again soon."

With that, we left the ball.

Tom was quiet on the journey back to the hotel. I wondered if it was because of what had happened earlier with Anton. When we were back in the room, I asked him what was wrong.

"Nothing, I'm fine. Did you enjoy tonight?"

"It was ok... different."

Tom poured me a drink from the mini bar and handed it to me. "Different good or different bad?"

"Just different," I replied. I kicked my shoes off and climbed onto the bed, adjusting the pillows slightly so I could rest my head against the headboard.

"Well, I'm glad you enjoyed it," he said as he polished all of his drink off.

I stared back at him. "I didn't say I enjoyed it! Did you?"

Tom didn't reply, just shrugged his shoulders. What was wrong with him? He took me, I didn't ask to go. I didn't want to argue with him. I could do that at home. He came over and lay on his side next to me on the bed, resting his head on his hand. "So, was it good then...?"

"What? I don't know what you mean."

"You know, you and that bloke."

"I told you it wasn't anything really, just different. What's all this about? You were the one that took me remember."

With that, Tom grabbed me with some force, frantically pulling at the laces on the front of my dress. Once undone he pulled the fabric down, exposing my breasts. He clutched them hard, pressed his lips against mine and penetrated my mouth with his tongue. He roughly turned me over and pulled me down by my ankles, till my torso was at the foot of the bed. Pushing my dress up, he groaned as he saw my stockings. His lips touched the top of my naked thigh, he pulled at my lace pants and revealed my naked flesh.

His lips brushed against my skin, and slowly he traced them around my bottom. His fingers searched for my clitoris, gently teasing it as they made contact with the pulsating flesh. I began to breathe faster, begging him to get inside me.

“No, not yet. Now you wait for me.” But I couldn’t – no – didn’t want to. I wanted him right now.

“For God’s sake, Tom, do it now.” And that’s just what he did.

In no time he was inside me, fucking me hard from behind, thrusting me against the bed. With every move, I let out a sound of pleasure, and my heavy breathing soon turned into groans of anticipation.

My body craved him more and more. The rush built up; then, like a wave crashing over me, it was there. My body stiffened with the pleasure that engulfed me. Tom's rhythm gathered pace, faster and harder than ever before until he too cried out with pleasure.

We lay side by side afterwards. I wondered what he was thinking and then he broke the silence with, "I'm sorry."

"What for?" I replied.

"Everything. You're right, it was me who took you, but I was watching you tonight, and I couldn't stand to see you with anyone else."

I sat up and rested against the headboard. I wasn't expecting to hear that from him. I got up and went to the bathroom, locking the door behind me.

I could hear Tom calling through to me, "Alex, I'm sorry. I've ruined it now, haven't I? It wasn't meant to be like this. It was going to be fun, we said, didn't we?" He was asking and answering his own questions at the same time. I stood at the sink and looked at myself in the mirror, wondering what I was doing. He was right. This was never meant to happen. Since my meeting with Maria in Skiathos, my whole world had truly turned upside down.

When I came out of the bathroom, he was sat on the bed. "Are you ok?" he asked.

"Yes, I'm fine, just tired." I climbed into bed and beckoned him over. He climbed in next to me and we held each other close till we fell asleep.

The next morning, we went for breakfast as usual. Tom was

quiet though, and for once he seemed to be the one who was distant. "Is everything ok, Tom?"

"Yes, just thinking about some business I have to attend to, not looking forward to it."

I wasn't sure that I believed him. I wasn't sure what, but something had changed. Breakfast that morning was the quietest I had ever had with Tom. We were usually chatting constantly but not today.

CHAPTER FIFTEEN

My journey home took forever. I couldn't get Tom out of my head; I was confused, and my emotions were all over. What the hell was wrong with me? It was all supposed to be a bit of fun, nothing serious.

Everything was the same at home, James nursing his laptop and the boys constantly in and out, using the house like a hotel.

The weekend seemed to drag. I kept myself busy by immersing myself in gathering information for a business meeting I had the next week. I returned to work on Monday and endeavoured to catch up on the work I had neglected while I had been with Tom. Susan and Lily seemed to be boring me even more than usual, and I just wanted to get away from it all. How I longed to be on that beautiful island, my island... Skiathos.

My silence was broken by the sound of Susan's voice "Alex, Alex."

“What?”

“Oh, sorry, I was just going to say I’ve brought that book for you.”

“Sorry, Susan, it’s me. I was miles away. Just thinking about this meeting tomorrow.”

“Oh, right, that’s ok. Anyway, I’ll lend you this one, then if you like it, I can lend you the others.”

I reached over the desk and took the book from her. I ran my fingers over the front cover and wondered what the fuss was all about.

“You have to give it chance. It’s a bit slow to begin with,” exclaimed Lily.

I looked up at Susan and smiled. “Thanks, Susan, I’ll give it a try, and thanks, Lily. I will do.”

That night when I got home, I began to gather my things together for the business seminar I was due to attend in London the next day. I didn’t sleep well that night. I hadn’t heard from Tom and I wondered if everything was ok. I must have nodded off though, and the next thing I knew, my alarm had gone off. The snooze button seemed so tempting, and without realising, I had pressed it.

The first thing I remembered that morning was one of the boy's standing over me.

“Mum, can you drop us off at college?"

I glanced over at the clock and answered, "Sorry, guys, no chance. I'm running really late," I replied, then made my way down stairs. "James, why didn't you wake me?"

"Oh, sorry, I didn't know you had to be up," grunting at me as he said it.

"But you did. I told you last night, I have a business

meeting in London." I didn't wait for a reply. I don't expect I would have got one; he was too busy reading his paper.

I dashed back upstairs, grabbed a quick shower, and got myself ready in a hurry. I grabbed my phone and quickly checked it: still no word from Tom. I made my way to my car on the drive, inserted the key in the ignition but nothing happened. It wouldn't even turn over. Of all the times it had to fail me, it had to be now. I had no time to discover the reasons why; I had to get to the railway station.

I hurried back into the house and called for a taxi. It soon arrived, and as I headed out the door, I noticed the book Susan had lent me was still on the side. I grabbed it and threw it in my bag, thinking it would give me something to read on the train.

We arrived at the station in no time. I made my way over to the ticket office.

"Hi, could I have a return ticket to London please?"

"Certainly, Madam, that will be ninety-nine pounds please."

"I'm sorry, how much?!"

"Ninety-nine pounds."

"Are you kidding me? It can't be!"

"I'm afraid so. You see, if you had booked them in advance, you would have received a considerable discount, but unfortunately, you didn't, and therefore..."

I drifted off for a moment whilst watching his mouth move, unable to hear the words and not really wanting to. This was the last thing I needed at the moment.

"Madam...MADAM!" he called out to me.

I jumped back into the moment. "Yes?"

"Do you want the tickets or not? I have a large queue

forming behind you and the train leaves in five minutes."

"Yes, sorry. I do." I frantically searched in my purse for my credit card. *Please don't say I have left it.*

As the ticket seller annoyingly tapped his fingers on the counter, my eyes finally fell upon the familiar blue shade of the card. "Ah, here it is!"

"At last..." he mumbled.

I was relieved I had my card and extremely grateful that I still had some credit on it. I was always using it to help the boys out. I grabbed my ticket from the man behind the counter and boarded the train.

Despite the pricing, I was fortunate enough that the only tickets available were in business class. I felt I needed it today with all the hassle I'd had to endure.

I was nearly the last person on the train and I made my way to the business class carriages. These were comfortable areas, small compartments that held around four people comfortably.

In the first one I came to was two business men. I didn't fancy being in there with them on my own. I would have felt awkward, I think. In the next carriage was an attractive, smartly dressed business woman, probably around fifty something. She was sat on her own, dressed in a black skirt suit. She looked up and smiled at me. I slid open the door, stepped inside and smiled back at her.

I sat opposite and opened my briefcase to check I had all my paperwork before relaxing in the seat and breathed a sigh of relief.

About thirty minutes into the journey, the carriage door startled me as it opened.

"Tickets please."

I rifled through my bag, looking for my ticket. Meanwhile the smartly dressed woman reached into her bag and pulled out hers. The inspector checked it and handed it back to her.

"Thank you, Madam."

"You're welcome, young man," winking at him as she said it.

In an instant, I recognised her voice, but I couldn't place her face. I finally found my ticket and held it up to the inspector with satisfaction. He checked the ticket, scanned the barcode and left the carriage; no thank you for me.

Just then my phone rang. "Sorry, got to take this," I said. The office had contacted me to confirm some details regarding the meeting I was going to. I finished the call and apologised again. "Sorry about that; it was work."

"It's fine," she replied.

Her voice again rang bells; I just felt like I knew her. I relaxed back into the seat and gazed out of the window, wishing I could hear from Tom, even just to make sure he was alright.

Thinking of him reminded me that I had brought the book Susan had lent me to read on the train. I must have only got through the first chapter when I noticed out the corner of my eye that the woman in the carriage was staring at me. I glanced up at her and she smiled. I quickly smiled back at her and continued to read my book.

A little while later, I could hear her rummaging about in her handbag. I looked across and noticed she had produced a makeup compact. She began to check her makeup. Reaching back into her bag, she pulled out her lipstick. She slowly removed the lid, and whilst pouting her lips, she brushed it against them. Her eyes looked up and met my own over the top of her compact, and I quickly looked away. She took me by surprise as she said, "So, how are you, darling?"

"I'm sorry," I replied. "Do I know you?"

She laughed and threw her head back. "I believe we have met."

"Really, have we?"

"Yes, darling, at the masquerade ball."

It was the woman I was talking to on the decking area at the ball! "Oh yes, hi. I'm sorry I didn't recognise you without the mask. How did you know it was me?"

"My dear, I never forget a voice." She held out her hand and said, "Kathryn, and you?"

I took her hand. It was so soft, the type that had probably never done a hard day's work. "I'm Alexandra."

We began chatting, mainly about our jobs. I was surprised to discover that she was a solicitor.

"So, why are you so surprised that I'm a solicitor?"

"I'm not!"

"Come on now, I can see it in your eyes. We're only human, you know." She laughed and threw her head back again.

I felt embarrassed and wanted to leave the carriage, but I knew it wasn't an option.

"So, that was your first time at the masquerade ball then?"

There was no point lying as she would have known. I gathered a strand of hair that had strayed from the pin that was holding it up and clipped it back into position. "Yes, it was."

"So, who was your friend?"

I stumbled over what to say. "My partner."

She quickly glanced at my left hand. "Your partner! So not your husband then?"

I could feel myself going red. "No, no, not my husband."

She continued to ask me questions about my relationship with Tom, and I found myself telling her everything, right from my experience with Maria.

"My, you do lead a colourful life."

I laughed with embarrassment at her remark. "Well, not really. It's kind of snowballed."

"Really! Well, that's the kind of snow balls I like." We both laughed at her remark. "I see you're a Mr Grey fan."

"Who, sorry?"

"Mr Grey!" she replied and nodded at the book.

"Oh, this? Well, I wouldn't say a fan, I've just borrowed it from a friend to see what all the fuss is about really."

"And what do you think?"

"Well, not much up to now, but I've been told to give it a chance."

"Yes, that's right. It gets better."

"You've read it then?"

"I don't think there are many women out there that haven't."

"Well, it's all new to me."

"You don't say. Well, if you ask me, you sound like an old hand at it from the stories you've been telling me." I laughed nervously.

Kathryn got up from her seat. "I'm going for a coffee; would you like one?"

"Yes, a cappuccino would be lovely please."

She soon returned with two coffees in hand. I stood to grab the door and let her in. As she handed me the coffee, I glanced down at her hands to see if she was wearing a ring. She met my eyes as I looked back up.

"I'm not married, dear, but I do live with someone. We

have been together for fourteen years. I did the marriage thing, and it didn't work out. Too much commitment for my liking."

"But surely it's the same living with someone?"

"Hell no! We do our own thing, and he likes the sort of thing I do."

"Like what?"

"Well, the ball for instance."

"Oh, was he there?"

"Who, Anton? Yes, he loves it!" I nearly dropped my coffee as she said his name.

"Anton, that's an unusual name..."

"Yes, its Antonio. He's Italian."

I didn't know what to say to her, so I took another sip from my coffee and gazed into my lap.

"I met him at a club about fifteen years ago. He was still married, and my divorce was coming through."

"So, has he lived here long?"

"Since he was a teenager, about nineteen years. He's thirty-eight now." I must have looked startled. "And yes, he's my toy boy!" she laughed.

I didn't know what to say. I'm sure there couldn't have been more than one Anton there that evening. I was relieved to finally have arrived at my destination. "Well, it's been lovely talking to you, Kathryn."

"Yes, and you too. Here, let me give you my card. Call me sometime and we can meet up for coffee." I took the card from Kathryn and told her I would call, but somehow, I didn't think I would.

CHAPTER SIXTEEN

It was a short walk from the station to the hotel where the meeting was to be held. I checked in at the reception desk and was shown to the correct conference room by the concierge. I thought I had made good time, but all the other delegates were already seated, and the speaker was about to start. I tried to ease myself into the room with little disruption and was looked at sternly by a couple of people. I smiled and mouthed sorry as I moved along the back row and sat in the first empty seat I came to.

The rest of the morning seemed to drag on, and I found myself daydreaming about my weekend with Tom. In fact, I struggled to get the whole thing out of my head, especially now I knew about Kathryn and Anton. I was disturbed by the coughing of a large man sat behind me, which made me jump and brought me crashing back to reality.

At lunch time I looked for someone to share a table with. I could see Mavis Stockwell who was head of the research department in London, sat with John Wright who was the Regional Manager and thought he was every woman's answer to Mr Perfect, when in fact he was just annoying. He was average height, middle aged, with a middle-aged spread to match. I made my way over to join them.

John got up out of his seat as I arrived at the table and greeted me with a kiss on the cheek. I shuddered, and not with delight.

"Lovely to see you, Alex. How have you been?"

"Fine, thank you, John, and you?"

"I'm good, thank you. You've met Mavis before, haven't you?"

"Yes, of course I have. How are you, Mavis?"

Mavis just replied with a 'fine, thank you' and shrunk back into herself; she never had much to say. She was late forties but dressed a lot older than her years. I never knew how to take her. She always seemed quiet, but she could chair a meeting no problem.

"You're looking as lovely as ever, Alex. What have you been doing with yourself since I last saw you?"

"Oh, not much, John, just working. You know how it is!"

"Say, why don't we catch up over a drink tonight? Are you booked in at the hotel?"

"No, sorry, I'm not. Got to get back tonight. I'm back in at work tomorrow." *Thank goodness*, I thought. I couldn't have stood a night talking about work and trying to fight off his advances.

The afternoon was just as boring as the morning, and I was beginning to wish I hadn't made such an effort to get there, as I didn't feel it was worth it. Luckily, I managed to slip out before it ended, as I wanted to make sure I got back to the station on time.

When I got on the train, I found what I thought was a quiet carriage and I must have nodded off, waking only when somebody's garish ringtone started playing noisily, much to everyone's annoyance. Jeez, why can't people have some respect and leave their phones on silent when in enclosed public spaces? I was so tired. I'd been up early and chasing around to get to the most boring meeting. I just wasn't in the mood.

I glanced up at the offender, giving him the evil eye as he answered the call. I reached into my bag to look for the day's notes to read, in an attempt to distract me from the sound of his voice. I put them back in my bag after a few minutes. I wasn't in the right mood to digest them. As I opened my bag, I caught sight of Susan's book and pulled it out again to give it another try.

I managed to read another couple of chapters and wondered what all the fuss was about. I remembered Lily saying to give it a chance, so flicked through it until I reached something that caught my eye. Chapter seven seemed to be where it began. Some of the scenes did remind me a little of Tom. I wondered if he had read this book too and couldn't help but laugh to myself.

I arrived home around 9pm. I was pleased I could charge my expenses to work, what with all the taxis and trains. As I pulled up in the taxi, I noticed my car was gone and instead Sal's was on the drive. I loved Sal, but after the day I had, I wasn't sure that I felt like her company tonight.

I walked into the living room, finding James and Sal sat opposite one another on the sofas.

"Ah, here you are, Alex. I've been here since seven!"

"Well, sorry about that, Sal, but I thought James would have told you about my terrible morning, hence my late return. Where are the boys?"

"Oh, I think they're both at some friend's house, said they might not be in tonight, rehearsing or something."

One of the boys had recently decided to form a band. I couldn't knock it as I'd tried it with a couple of friends when I was at school. It was all good fun and something to reflect on later in life.

"Hmm, James, did mention you had a problem with the car."

"Oh yes, by the way, Alex, I phoned John at the garage. He picked your car up today and said he should be able to get it back to you by Friday. He's going to ring tomorrow and let you know what is wrong with it and give you a quote."

"Great. Well, if you don't mind, Sal, I'm going to nip for a shower and head off to bed. It's been a long day." I wasn't in the mood for small talk. I leant over the couch, gave her a kiss on the cheek and headed for the door.

"Ok, hun, no worries. I'll text you tomorrow." I felt a little guilty after Sal had been waiting there for so long, but I was really exhausted and needed my bed.

As I entered the kitchen the next morning, James was full of it. Not in a bad way, he just seemed unusually happy.

"I meant to tell you last night, Jack rang to invite us to a party round at theirs on Friday night. I said we would go."

The thought of spending an evening with Jack and Sarah constantly sniping at each other filled me with dread, especially as I would probably get stuck with Sarah as she didn't have many other close friends.

"Huh, you did, did you? What if I don't want to go?"

"Don't go then. I just thought it would be a nice change. We haven't been out with them for ages. I mentioned it to Sal as well last night, and she said she fancies it."

Well, no change there, I thought. Sal won't turn a party down. "How come you've asked Sal? She hardly knows them." Not that I was bothered; at least I would have someone else to talk to.

"Well, she sounded a bit down, so I said she could come with us. Besides, they won't mind."

I don't think James had a clue about what was going on with Jack and Sarah. Sometimes he couldn't see what was going on right in front of him, although I would have thought Jack would have mentioned it to him.

CHAPTER SEVENTEEN

Friday night came all too soon. James was in from work unusually early, and after tea, he was first in the shower. The boys were out. We didn't seem to see much of them these days.

Oliver, or Olly as he liked to be known, was sticking it out with the band. While Daniel, or should I say Dan, wanted to concentrate on getting into university, which I was pleased about. I would have loved Oliver to do the same, but at the moment he was following his dream. I'm sure it will come one day.

I had grabbed a coffee and settled on the sofa to catch up on the news when James came down.

"Come on then, aren't you getting ready?" In all honesty, I wasn't that bothered about going to this party. I really just fancied staying in with a glass of wine and a good book. "I said we would be there at 7.30, and its nearly seven now."

I glanced up at James, took a sip from my coffee and

made my way up to the bedroom. I searched through my wardrobe for something to wear. I came across a distressed pair of jeans and decided to wear those, then managed to find a top that would complement them nicely. I quickly rummaged through my underwear draw for something to go underneath and headed for the shower.

In no time, I was out and ready. I managed to not get my hair wet. I couldn't be bothered to wash it.

James shouted up from downstairs. "How you are doing up there?"

"Yes, I'm nearly ready." I popped a bit of eyeliner and mascara on, blushed my cheeks up and was ready to go.

When I came downstairs, James was already making his way out the door. "Come on!"

I slipped some heels on and followed him out.

When we arrived at Jack and Sarah's, there were already a few people there, but no sign of Sal. Jack came to greet us. "Alex, glad you could make it. You look lovely as ever."

James made some brief small talk with Jack and then went to find Sal. I made my way into the kitchen to make myself a drink and then went back into the hallway. I was surprised to see so many people. I wasn't expecting that. I wondered if they were mostly work colleagues.

I took a seat on one of the stairs, sipped my wine and waited for Sal to appear. While I was sitting there, Sarah came down the stairs. "Alex, so glad you could make it."

We exchanged a kiss on the cheek, and I moved over slightly so she could sit beside me. She seemed a lot happier. Sarah said that she and Jack had been getting on better lately. I was pleased for her, although I had some reservations. I felt it was probably false on Jack's part as he was not to be trusted.

After a short while, Sarah got called away to talk to somebody else, and I was once again alone on the stairs. James came through into the hallway with a drink in hand. "Ah, there you are. I've been looking for you. I can't see Sal anywhere."

"Maybe she didn't fancy it."

"Hmm, still not like her to turn down a party though."

We sat there in silence for a while. I didn't know what to say to him. In the background, someone had put some jazz music on. I turned to James and said, "I like sax."

"I'm surprised to hear you say that."

"Why, what do you mean?"

"You saying that you like sex!"

I began laughing out loud. "I didn't!"

"Well, yes, you did, just now!"

"No, I said I like sax! The saxophone." We both began to laugh. I thought to myself, *Actually, I do like sex, James. It's just you never took the time to share it much with me.*

My thought was suddenly disturbed as Jack came over to us. "So, how's my favourite couple then?"

"Fine, thanks, and you?"

"Yes, I'm good, Alex. Busy with work and that. What have you been up to?" With that, James deserted me again as he caught sight of Sal coming through the door.

"Erm, I've not been up to much really, Jack."

He squeezed up beside me on the stairs, and once again I felt uncomfortable around him. I thought the world of Sarah.

She was a lovely person who would do anything for anyone, a little annoying at times, but then again who isn't?

"So, where have you been going on your nights away?"

I quickly turned to look at him, and I felt myself going red. "What? I haven't got a clue what you're on about."

"I mean your overnight stays. Where do you go?"

I clenched my wine glass and took a large gulp from it. "Not that it's any business of yours, but I have had to attend several business meetings."

Jack tossed his head back and laughed at me. "As if you would be up to anything."

Just for a minute, I wanted to tell him, just let him know that I had been up to more than he could imagine. Well, maybe not, but more than he would ever imagine that I would do. I had to stop myself, but I did just want him to know. He turned and stroked my cheek. "Oh, my dear Alex." I could feel the hairs on my neck rising. He made me shudder. I half-smiled at him, quickly got up and walked away.

I made my way into the kitchen to join James and Sal. "Hi, Al, how's it going?" She winked at me as she said it.

"Yeah, I'm good thanks. What about you?"

"I'm fine. James was telling me you've had a lot of work away, what was it, seminars?"

I looked up at Sal and couldn't believe she had said it. What was with everyone tonight? "Yes, that's right. We're very busy at work and I seem to have drawn the short straw."

Sal smiled at me as she took another sip of her wine as James disappeared to mingle. She let out a loud laugh. "You handled that well, Alex."

"You're unreal. Why did you do that?"

"Your face was a picture!"

I shook my head and couldn't help but laugh at what she had done. "So, how is Mr Grey?"

"He's fine, thank you."

"And when is your next meeting?"

"Look, can we change the subject please?"

"No, I'm interested on how things are going."

"Well..."

Just then Sarah came into the kitchen. I've never been so pleased to see her. "Great party, Sarah! Thanks for inviting us."

"No problem, glad you're enjoying it!"

She started talking to Sal, so I slipped away. In all honesty, I wasn't in the mood for a party and I felt like I should go. I found James and told him I wanted to leave. He clearly didn't want to, so I told him just to stay and that I would see him when he got back. I slipped out of the door and waited for my taxi on the front. I very much doubted anyone would miss me.

CHAPTER EIGHTEEN

The weekend passed quickly. James nursed his hangover and I didn't really do anything. I couldn't be bothered. By the time Monday morning arrived, I realised I still hadn't heard anything from Tom. Susan and Lily were nattering on about a load of rubbish, and I was just nodding in the right places– at least I hoped I was.

My boredom was interrupted by the sound of my phone, signalling I had received a message. It was Tom.

Can you make it this weekend?

I wanted to reply instantly, my heart was pounding, but I felt I should make him wait. I slipped my phone back into my bag.

"Anyone interesting?" remarked Lily.

"No, just Oliver." I could feel my skin colouring up as I said it. I read the same line on my computer about four times before I realised it was no good; I had to text him back.

Yes, possibly, I will let you know later today.

I knew that I could make it, but I mustn't seem too keen.

OK, can you let me know by 5 so I can get things sorted?

I'm guessing "things" meant he had to make his excuses to his wife.

I texted Tom back around three that afternoon and told him I would be there. When I got home, I told James that I was going to visit my friend again at the weekend.

"Yes, you should go see how she's coping without her husband."

Well, that was relatively easy, I thought. He didn't seem to bat an eyelid.

I had a really busy week at work, trying to get on top of all my jobs before the weekend so I didn't have to think about them while I was away.

I was sat at my desk trying to complete one of my research papers when I was interrupted by Susan.

"So how are you getting on with Mr Grey then?"

I looked up from my desk in shock, wondering how she could know. Susan stared at me in anticipation of my reply.

I stumbled for the right words to say. "I... Erm, well I... Erm, don't know what you mean." I felt myself going red as I said it

"The book, Alex, what do you think?"

A wave of relief rushed over me – the book! "Oh, the book! Well, yes, it's ok, I did skip a few pages though."

"So which chapter are you on?"

"I think I'm about to start chapter eight."

"Ooh, you're in for a treat, isn't she, Lily?"

"Yes, stick with it. You won't believe what they get up to!" *Somehow, I think I will,* I thought.

"My husband reckons it's changed our marriage. What about you, Lily?"

Lily just blushed a little and turned back to face her computer.

"He said he's never had so much." I listened as Susan proceeded to tell me the intimate details of her sex life, which I felt was a bit too much information.

As the afternoon wore on, I decided I needed a drink, so I texted Sal to see what she was up to.

Hi Sal, any chance we could meet up after work for a drink?

She replied straight away.

Yeah sure, is everything okay?

Yes, all good, I just need a chat!

Okay then, I'll see you in our usual place about 6.00.

See you later!

I messaged James as well to let him know I wouldn't be in till late, but just got the usual okay from him.

. . .

I left the office around five thirty and made my way into the centre of town. I had been walking for around ten minutes when I was caught in a torrential shower, and as usual I didn't have a brolly with me. I began to run, looking up at the sky and hoping it would ease up soon. As I struggled along in my heels, I suddenly stumbled, falling sideways and crashing into an athletic-looking man as he made his way out of Marks & Spencer's. I wanted to swear but managed to contain it to a grunt under my breath.

"Are you okay?" he asked.

"Yes, thank you, I'm fine."

"Are you sure? You look a bit shook up."

"No, really, I'm good, thank you." I quickly composed myself and carried on up the street.

I reached the wine bar looking like a drowned rat. Sal was already sat at the table, looking like she had just stepped off the catwalk as usual.

"Oh my, is it raining?" I looked up at her and glared. She began to laugh. "Did you not bring a brolly?"

"Oh yeah, I just chose not to use it." We both laughed.

Sal poured me a glass of wine from the half-drunk bottle on the table. I took a large mouthful and sank back into my chair. "I needed that."

"I'm guessing you've had a bad day?"

"No, not really... Well, Susan has driven me mad as usual, and I thought she had found out about Tom."

"Why, what did she say?"

"Well, she asked how Mr Grey was..."

Sal nearly spat her drink out as I told her. "So, what did you say?"

"Well, I stumbled a bit, then she said, 'You know, the book.'" Sal fell about laughing. "You see, I borrowed the book off her. Anyway, I'm glad you think it's funny! I was mortified!"

"Oh, Alex, I would love to have seen your face!" I smiled back at her and took another sip of wine. "I'm just off to the loo, Al, won't be a min."

I reached into my bag for my compact to check what sort of state I was in. I stared into the mirror. With my panda eyes and my hair stuck to my head, I wasn't a pretty sight. I grabbed my wipes out of my bag and fixed my face as best I could, added a bit of lippy and felt much better.

As I closed my compact and looked up, I noticed a guy at the bar staring at me. I thought I recognised him then I realised it was the guy who I fell onto in the street. I looked away embarrassed, but I could see he was making his way towards me. "Hi, I'm Will. We met in the..."

I quickly interrupted him. "Yes, I know where we met."

"I must say, you managed to recover yourself well. It could have been a lot worse if you had hit the floor." I couldn't help but laugh as I thought about me hurtling towards him like a bull charging at a matador. "So, how come your in here alone?"

"I'm not, my friend has just gone to the loo." "Friend! Male or female?"

"Female."

"Oh, so are you single?"

"No, no, I'm not. I'm married." And god knows I couldn't

do with anymore complications in my life. "Oh, that's a shame. I'm looking for a girlfriend."

"Then look no further," a voice came from behind us; it was Sal. "So, who's this, Alex?"

"Erm, this is Will; Will this is Sal."

"Hi, Sal, nice to meet you."

"Hmm and you," Sal said as she held her hand out to shake his. She had that look in her eye. Bless him, he didn't stand a chance.

"Will you excuse me, ladies, while I go to the bathroom?"

"Sure, I'll hold your drink for you." She grabbed the drink from out of his hand as he turned to go to the loo.

"So, you kept him quiet. Where did you meet? I want all the details!"

"I fell on him in the rain."

"What! When?"

"Tonight, on my way here."

Sal started to laugh again. "Well, that's one way of meeting someone. I must say you did okay! He's gorgeous!"

He was rather handsome and very fit looking. I'm guessing he worked out on a regular basis. He had light brown hair and was unshaven, which gave him a bit of a rugged look.

My thoughts drifted back into the conversation, and I realised what Sal had just said.

"Oh no, I'm not interested in him!"

"Good, that leaves it open for me. Besides, you have Mr Grey."

I was just about to give her what for when I was interrupted. "So, do you both come here a lot?"

"Yes, we do, don't we, Al?"

"Well, we haven't been for a while, but yes, it is our usual haunt."

The conversation naturally flowed between us all night. Will seemed to be a nice guy, a bit full of himself, but he was okay. I had a feeling he had been a bit insecure at some time and his current image was to mask his insecurities. Sal seemed to be into him and was lapping up his charm. It turned out he was new to the area – something to do with his job. I wasn't really listening, but I kept catching bits of the conversation. My mind was elsewhere. I was looking forward to my meeting with Tom, and tomorrow couldn't come fast enough.

I woke the next day at around 7am, made my way downstairs and enjoyed the peace and quiet with the paper and a coffee. I thought about what I could wear for my weekend away with Tom. I didn't want to go rummaging about while James was in the bedroom, but at least I could work out what I was going to wear.

It wasn't long before James came down and interrupted my peace. "You're up early?"

"I woke up and couldn't get back over to sleep so thought I might as well get up."

"Okay, do you want another coffee?"

"Yes, can do. I'm just going to nip up and pack my bag."

"Oh yes, you're going to Jen's for the weekend, aren't you?"

"Yes, I'll just go throw some things in a bag and I'll be back down."

I made my way up to the bedroom and searched for something to wear. I should have bought something new. I managed to find a dress I had never worn and popped it in my overnight bag, along with some stockings. I was really looking forward to seeing Tom. I had missed him so much.

I made my way back downstairs, and James had a coffee waiting for me. I sat opposite him at the table and watched as he trawled his way through his newspaper, hardly noticing I was there.

Suddenly he looked up. "What's wrong?"

"Nothing."

"Then why are you staring?"

"I wasn't, I was just looking at you."

"And?"

"And nothing."

"So, I haven't changed then." James started to laugh and continued to read his paper.

No, James you haven't changed, I thought. *You're just the same as you have always been.* I took another sip from my coffee cup and wondered how we ever got this far, both work-obsessed and only really spending time together whilst on holiday. I thought maybe that's what had saved us, the fact that we were so preoccupied with work we didn't have much time to spend together. I guess some people are like that. They just drift along with the tide.

I rose from my chair. "Would you like some toast?"

Without even looking up, James replied, "Two slices please."

I made us some toast and a fresh coffee and sat back down at the table, wondering what the weekend had in store for me. I looked out of the window. The sky had turned grey and rain was drumming against the window.

That's all I needed. I glanced up at the clock. It was time I was going, so I finished getting ready and headed for the car.

By the time I reached the motorway, the rain was beating down and it was difficult to see in front of me. I decided to pull in at a services until it calmed down. I purchased a coffee at the counter and searched for a seat. It seems everyone had had the same idea as the place was packed, I couldn't find anywhere to sit.

I was just about to give up when a voice called out. "You can sit with me if you like, dear." I turned to face the table behind me, and I was surprised to see James's mum staring back at me. "Well, this is a surprise. What are you doing here?"

"I, erm, I'm on my way to see my friend, and you?"

"I'm going to see Aunt Edith." Edith was Joan's sister and they often visited each other. "And how is James? I haven't seen him for a while."

"Oh, he's fine, working as hard as ever."

"He never stops, that boy. He will run himself into the ground."

We chatted for a while over our coffee until the rain had cleared, then as soon as I could, I said my goodbye's and left. Tom would be waiting for me, I thought, and I can't wait for him.

I reached the hotel a little later than our arranged time, and I was a little surprised that Tom wasn't already there. He was never late. It was a little early for alcohol, so I ordered a soft drink from the bar and made my way to the sofa in the main foyer. I grabbed one of the magazines neatly placed on the table and began to flick through it.

Halfway through an article on the latest movie releases, I glanced down at my watch. I had been there thirty minutes, where was he? This wasn't like him at all. Just then I received a text on my phone.

Really sorry, unable to make it, something has cropped up x.

I was so annoyed. What a time to tell me!

Like what?!

The bloody cheek of it, letting me know now.

I'm truly sorry, I can't speak now. I'll be in touch x.

He couldn't even spare me an explanation. I looked down at my phone, wondering if that was it. Maybe he couldn't do it anymore and couldn't face telling me. *What a coward,* I thought. *I've a good mind to text him back and tell him where to go.*

I began to write a lengthy message, adding that it was good while it lasted, but I was happy to finish it now as I had had enough. I paused before sending then decided to delete it. What was the point? He had probably done it time and time again.

The journey home seemed to take forever, and I'm not ashamed to say I was disappointed. I was really pissed off that Tom had not turned up. We had such a good night planned.

Then suddenly, I felt a pang of guilt. Here I was moaning about missing out on my night while Tom may be dealing with some emergency. I hoped everything was alright and it wasn't anything serious.

James's car was in the drive when I got home. How would I explain my early return? Maybe I could just say my friend had an emergency. After all, it was nearly true, just wasn't the friend he was thinking of.

I left my overnight bag in the hall and made my way through to the lounge. There was no James. *He may have gone out*, I thought. I needed a drink. I knew there was a bottle of Prosecco in the fridge but couldn't see it. Damn, James must have beaten me to it. I decided to go and have a bath instead.

I scanned the kitchen before I turned out the light to head upstairs, and something caught my eye. There were two wine glasses on the breakfast bar. *That was unusual,* I thought. James was fanatical about using too many pots when not needed. I smiled to myself; maybe he was feeling reckless.

I made my way upstairs. As I reached the last few steps, I noticed a light shining from under our bedroom door. I imagined James would be sat in bed clutching his laptop, checking his work.

I thought I could hear voices but was quick to dismiss it as the television in the bedroom. As I grew closer, I recognised James's voice. He was groaning in a way I had never heard him before, well, at least not with me. A sick, empty feeling surfaced in the pit of my stomach. I couldn't believe it, I couldn't focus, and I just couldn't take it in. James was having an affair.

I reached the top step and froze, sinking my bottom onto

the stair, resting my head against the bannister with tears streaming down my face. I struggled to stifle the sounds I was making. Why, why would he do this to me? And with who? And why bring her to our bed?

I tried to piece things together in my head, like when did this start and how? In all honesty, it wasn't too difficult. James had worked long hours and late nights for years, or had he? Wait, what was I thinking? What had I been doing with Tom for the last few months? But that was different. Well, it certainly wasn't an affair; it was just sex, wasn't it? My head was spinning, how could I even think that was acceptable?

My mind continued to argue with itself, and all the time in the distance, James continued to give it to her like he had never given it to me. I decided it was no good; I had to confront them. I would walk in, throw her out, and we would discuss what we had both done. I would tell James everything and we would try to sort this terrible mess out.

I stood in front of the door shaking from head to toe, ready to burst in, my heart pounding like a drum. I stopped. Would I be able to live with the memory of James with another woman for the rest of my life? How could I live with that image in my mind? Should I just walk out the door and leave him to his new life? No, I couldn't and why should I? Surely twenty-four years together counted for something.

I stood there a wreck. A mad rage swept over me, and before I knew it, I had opened the door.

CHAPTER NINETEEN

No one could have prepared me for what was behind that door.

I flung the door open, and two shocked faces stared back at me, two people I knew very well. I couldn't believe they had done this to me. How could they? I trusted them, and they betrayed me, both of them.

The shock for me was too much. I rushed to the bathroom and began to vomit. James followed me. I felt his hand on my shoulder as he tried to comfort me.

"Alex..."

"Get off me! Leave me alone!" I continued to be sick.

"I'm sorry, Alex, sorry you had to find out like this." He put his hand back on my shoulder and moved my hair away from my face.

"I said leave me alone! You disgust me!" I yelled.

"We didn't plan this, it just happened. There was an attraction we couldn't fight, and I'm sorry, truly sorry."

I stood up and made my way to the sink, splashing cold

water on my face. James sat on the edge of the bath with his head in his hands and began to sob. The pitiful cries that came from him had me almost cradling him like a baby, soothing him, telling him it would all be alright. But then my thoughts were drawn to the other person in my room, and in our bed. How could they?

I looked across at James. "How long?"

"Alex, don't do this. It doesn't matter how long."

"Do you know, James, you're right, that's the least of my worries. Why? That's what I want to know, why?"

James hung his head in shame and shrugged his shoulders. I could hear our friend in the background, scrambling around for their clothes on the bedroom floor. I turned around to leave the bathroom, and James caught my arm. "Alex, let me explain."

"How could you possibly explain this?" In the distance I could hear laughing. I broke away from James and made my way back to the bedroom, a rage engulfing me. I stood in the doorway feeling exhausted, yet fuelled with adrenalin, and I glared at the person who had been sleeping with my husband.

Before I even had chance to speak, they said, "Oh, if it isn't Miss Frigid."

I couldn't wait to deliver a reply and with a rawness in my voice I answered back, "Actually I'm not frigid. I'm wilder than you could ever imagine, but that's something you will never experience, Jack."

I turned around and made my way down the stairs. I could hear Jack laughing in the background. James followed me. "Alex, can we talk?"

I looked at him, a pathetic figure, dressed just in his underwear, who looked so lonely and I wondered how it had come to this. I wondered if he realised that Jack was a player and couldn't be trusted. I wondered if he even knew how many times Jack had tried it on with me, but most of all, I wondered when he realised he was gay.

"Alex, I'm talking to you."

"You're talking to me! I've been talking to you for the last twenty-four years and wanting you to listen, but you continuously peered at me over your newspaper or with your gaze fixed on your laptop." I continued down the staircase and made my way into the kitchen. I reached for the kettle and checked it for water before flicking the switch on and leaning against the work surface.

James slumped onto the stairs and held his head in his hands. I glanced around the room remembering the laughter from the boys and the mess they would leave the kitchen in. And then I caught sight of the two wine glasses and once again I felt sick. I angrily picked them up and slammed them into the sink, smashing them to pieces.

James entered the kitchen. "Alex!" he shouted. I just glared back at him. How dare he shout at me, judge my anger! He sat at the table. "Let's talk, Alex, we need to talk."

I blinked back the tears I could feel welling up again. "What would be the point of that?"

James moved towards me. "Please, just let me explain."

I held my hand up in front of me. "Don't come any closer." I pushed past him and made my way into the living room.

Just then I heard Jack come down the stairs. "Does this mean you need to find a hotel for the night, JJ?" He laughed as he said it.

"No, just go, Jack. I need to talk to Alex."

"Sure, you don't want me to hold your hand?" "No, I'll be fine."

I could still hear Jack in the distance. "Patronising bastard," I mumbled to myself. I stormed into the hallway. "Just get out, Jack. Now!"

He laughed. "Your face was a picture," he said as he left, closing the door behind him. I wanted to slap him. Instead I sunk on my knees to the floor and sobbed. James rushed forward to help me up.

"Get off! Just leave me, just leave me alone." I sobbed uncontrollably, somewhat like a baby.

Later, as I began to calm down, I could hear James crying. I assumed he was in the living room. I dragged myself to my feet and entered the kitchen. I flicked the kettle on again and went to the sink to wash my hands. It was full of glass, a result of my anger earlier. I carefully gathered as many pieces as possible and placed them in the bin. I made myself a coffee and sat at the table.

I wondered what time it was. I looked up at the clock – ten past seven – well, they didn't waste much time getting into bed after I left. I felt my stomach turn over at the thought of it. So, that's why James hadn't touched me for so long. A single tear rolled down my cheek. How could there be any more? I thought I was all cried out. I rested my head on the table, numbed by the whole thing. I suddenly thought about the boys, about what I would tell them, and began to cry again. What a mess.

James entered the kitchen and I quickly wiped the tears from my eyes "Oh, hi, JJ," I said sarcastically.

"Don't, Alex."

"Huh, JJ! Where the hell did that come from?"

"He's always called me it since Uni."

"Well, never in front of me!"

"No, it was a private thing."

"Huh, I bet it was!"

"So, you've been shagging since Uni then, eh?"

"Alex!"

"Sorry does that offend you?!"

"It's just not you, Alex, that's all."

"Funny that, JJ, because there's a lot we don't seem to know about each other."

James sat at the table opposite me. "What are you going to do?"

"Well, I thought we could freshen up and go for a meal somewhere, what do you think?" James looked up at me despairingly. "I don't know, James. I don't even know who I am anymore."

We sat in silence for a while until I eventually got up from the table and announced I was going for a bath. As it began to fill, I looked around for something to add. I grabbed the first bottle I came across. As I poured it in, the smell of jasmine filled the air and my time with Maria came flooding back to me. My head was so messed up with the events of the day: first Tom not turning up, then coming home to this.

I wondered how Tom was and what was so bad that he couldn't meet me. Surely his day couldn't be as eventful as mine! I realised I knew very little about Tom, apart from what he liked in the bedroom. But if only he had turned up, everything would have been fine. I would have never known anything about James, and we could have all carried on as we were. *But is that what I really wanted,* I asked myself, *to continue to live a lie?* I didn't know anymore. I didn't know what to think. I really just wanted to get away.

After a long soak, I grabbed my bathrobe and made my way to the bedroom. The bed was in disarray from its recent occupants. James' clothes were strewn all over the room, and Jack's watch lay on the bedside table. I turned away hastily to face the wardrobe instead and tried to chase the visions from my mind.

I quickly found something to wear, made myself look presentable, picked my jacket up and the weekend bag which was still packed. *That should do me for a couple of days,* I thought.

James met me in the hallway. "Alex, where are you going?"

"I don't know."

"But we need to talk."

"Not now, James, I can't." I walked out of the house and made my way to the car.

I sat in the car, wondering where I could go. I could see James stood at the front door. I searched for my mobile; I hoped I hadn't left it in the house. I found it in the bottom of my bag. No messages from Tom; he was long gone. I dialled Sal's number instead and waited for her to pick up. It was ringing for a while and just as I was about to hang up, she answered.

"Hi, Al, how's it going?" I burst into tears.

"Al, what's wrong?"

I couldn't speak. I was wailing again like a child.

"Alex, take a deep breath and speak to me."

I managed only a few words. "I need somewhere to stay."

"Oh, shit, James knows. Al, just go to mine now and I'll go straight home. Just wait if I'm not there."

"Ok, I will," I cried through pitiful sobs. I threw my phone on the seat, started the car and inched off the drive onto the street. I could still see James on the doorstep in the rear-view mirror.

CHAPTER TWENTY

I drove over to Sal's house on autopilot. There was no car outside, so she must still be on her way. I picked up my phone. I wanted to ring Tom and tell him everything. I wanted him to hold me and tell me it would be ok. I found his number and was just about to call him when Sal pulled up. She came running up to the car, opened my door, and as I got out, she held me tight. Once again I began to cry.

"Oh, you poor love, come on, let's get you in."

Sal put the kettle on. Her house was very different to ours, typical of a single person. Not a thing out of place. In fact, it hardly looked lived in. Knowing Sal, it probably wasn't.

" So, come on, how did he find out?" I looked at Sal and shook my head. "So, what?! Did you just tell him?"

I shook my head again. "No, Sal, it was James. He's been having the affair."

"You're kidding me!" Again, I shook my head. "Who with? Someone from work?"

"No, a close friend of ours."

"Oh my God, not Sarah!"

"No, not Sarah." I paused before I continued with my reply. "It's Jack."

I thought Sal was about to choke, but then she started laughing. "You're really having me on now!"

"I wish I was, Sal, but I'm not. It's true."

Sal stared in disbelief at me and sank into the chair opposite. With a stunned look in her eyes, she shook her head. "Well then," she said as she rose to her feet, "forget the coffee!" She opened her fridge which was largely stocked with wine and grabbed the nearest bottle.

We began to drink. I cried some more and so did Sal. we dissected James and Jack piece by piece. James repeatedly tried to call me which I continued to ignore, but I heard nothing from Tom.

The next day, Sal had plans and I couldn't interfere with them, that wouldn't be fair, so I just stayed in. I didn't feel like facing anyone, although I wondered how the boys were and what their father had told them. Sal had suggested that I go away for a couple of weeks. She even offered to lend me the money, bless her, but I fortunately had my emergency savings. Some that James didn't know about.

I went into work on the Monday and briefly explained the situation to my boss, omitting the finer details. She granted me a month off work which I was grateful for. To be fair, I had put in plenty of hours in the past, so I didn't feel like I was taking advantage.

Lily and Susan were huddled together over the desk

when I returned from the boss's office. I know their minds would have been working overtime. They loved a bit of gossip and this would have been like the jackpot for them. I didn't want to walk out without speaking at all, so I said I would be off for a few weeks due to personal reasons. That would keep them guessing till I got back.

When I left work that day, I returned to what I now loosely called home. As I entered the house, Oliver came into the hall. "Mum, where have you been? Dad's not well. He didn't go into work."

"Didn't he?" James obviously hadn't told them anything about what had happened. I was angry; he never explained anything to the boys, always left it to me. I wanted to blurt it all out, tell them the truth, but what would that solve. "Oliver, come into the kitchen, I've got something to tell you."

James suddenly appeared in the kitchen, unshaven and dishevelled. He looked dreadful. "Alex, don't do this please."

"Don't panic, James. Oliver, your dad and I are separating."

Oliver was so shocked, bless him. "What? Why?"

"We just don't love each other anymore."

James began to cry. "Oh, Alex, that's not true."

I glared across at James. "Don't push it, JJ."

Oliver looked confused. He was blinking away the tears. I moved towards him to cradle him in my arms, but he pushed me away. "So why don't you love dad anymore?! Have you found someone else?"

His comments broke me, and my emotions welled up once again. I sunk back into the chair and looked back at James unable to speak.

"Well, Mum?"

James finally stepped in. "It's not that, Ollie. We're just going to have a break and see how it goes."

I wiped both hands over my eyes and rose from the chair. "Sorry, I have to pack."

Oliver barged past me and ran up to his room, his door slammed behind him. As I entered the bedroom everything was the same. Jack's watch still lay on the bedside table. I grabbed my case from the top of the wardrobe and began to pack. My holiday items were still in it; I just added my bare essentials.

I heard James enter the room. "So where are you going, Alex?"

"I'm not just thinking about it, James. What did you say that for?"

"What!"

"We're having a break see how it goes!"

"Well, I thought if we..."

I interrupted him sharply. "We're finished, James. We can never go back, the damage is done."

"Alex, no, please. I love you!"

I scooped my toiletries up, put them in the case and zipped it up. Just then, Oliver came in. "See Mum, it is you. Dad loves you, he just said, I heard him."

I turned to Oliver. "Ollie, I'm so sorry, sweetheart. I just hope he tells you the truth one day."

"What, that you don't care anymore and you're leaving us?"

I moved forward to hug him, and he moved away, so I grabbed my case and made my way downstairs instead, leaving Oliver crying in his father's arms. Struggling to hold back the tears, I made my way out the door.

. . .

The next few days were a bit of a blur. I wrote letters to my boys, telling them how much I loved them and explaining as much as I could without going into the finer details. I just hoped that one day they would understand what had happened between me and their father, and I wanted to believe that he would sometime soon tell them the truth.

I saw a solicitor and started proceedings. I know it may have seemed a bit hasty, but it turned out that James and Jack had been carrying on together since Uni. I could never love him in that way again. If anything, he would be more like a friend now.

I'd had no news from Tom either. I hadn't bothered to text him, and there was no point. I knew where I stood. He had probably started his visits to Secret Dreams again to find his next conquest.

Once I had finally put things in place, I decided to go to Skiathos for a couple of weeks. I just needed to clear my head.

CHAPTER TWENTY-ONE

That week I boarded a plane to Greece. It was strange going there alone; I had always visited with James and the boys in the past. It was only in the last couple of years that we had started to go on our own.

I checked into our usual hotel. Everyone was pleased to see me but were naturally asking where James was. I didn't want to have to explain to them, so I just said he was back home working.

The next day, I woke early and opened the patio doors to the balcony. Although it felt strange being there alone, it felt good to be back. I looked out, and as the sea rushed onto the shore, I felt like I was home.

After breakfast I picked up my book, or should I say Susan's book, and found myself a sunbed. Reading it reminded me of Tom. Sal was right, he was somewhat like Mr Grey, and as the sun kissed my skin my senses heightened as I thought of him.

. . .

That afternoon I decided to have a walk to the beach. I found myself thinking about Maria and wondering what she was doing now. I wandered along the beach, passing the sunbeds where we met. I continued until I reached Maria's shack. I noticed the door was slightly ajar, but I couldn't see anyone around, and I didn't have the nerve to knock.

As I walked away, I heard my name being called.

"Alex!"

I turned in the direction the voice had come from. Maria stood in the doorway, her bronze skin accentuated by the long white skirt she was wearing, and a white cotton shirt which donned her shoulders and tied under her breasts in a tight knot.

"Hi..." I replied nervously. She came out to greet me with a kiss on each cheek.

"How are you?"

"I'm fine, thank you, and you?"

"Oh, I am good, busy you know, but that's good. Yes! Come in we will have a drink." Maria beckoned me into the shack. "You would like a wine?"

"Erm, no, could I have a coffee please?" "Frappe?"

"Yes, that would be lovely, thank you." I thought back to the last time I had drank wine with Maria; maybe it wasn't such a good idea.

We chatted again like old friends until we eventually came around to the day we first met.

"Why did you leave so suddenly that day?"

"It was late, my husband would wonder where I was."

"So, it was nothing else?"

"No, why?"

"I thought I had offended you."

"No not at all!" I felt myself blushing. "You see it never happened before; I hadn't done anything like that until then."

"No, me neither!"

We both laughed nervously at our embarrassment. So, Sal was wrong I thought. It wasn't what Maria did all the time.

As we immersed ourselves in conversation, I found myself telling her all about Tom and what James had been up to. I watched as her eyes widened. I wondered if she believed me. I'm not so sure I would.

We were interrupted by an attractive, sculpted man, who filled the frame of the door way. He was unshaven and had the most amazing warm eyes. Maria interrupted my train of thought. "Alex, this is Stavros, my husband."

I rose from the chair to shake his hand, then was quickly reminded we were in Greece. He held my hand and kissed me on either cheek. "Yassou," he said.

Maria laughed and said he was teasing and could speak perfect English. He asked if I would like to stay for tea but I declined. As lovely as the offer was, I felt I couldn't stay and make small talk with the man whose wife I had slept with a few months ago. I promised I would drop by again before I went back to England.

On my way back to the hotel, I couldn't help but feel relieved that I had not been so gullible on the day I met Maria, and that the whole thing was a new experience for us both. I felt my life was like shifting sands at the moment, not knowing which direction it was going to take.

. . .

That evening I made my way to our small bar at the edge of the beach. Dimitrious brought me my usual drink, and as the sun was setting, I looked out to sea. My head was all over the place, recalling the last few months. It had been a real roller coaster. One I could never have imagined.

There had been so many changes in such a short time. It dawned on me how little I knew about the people closest to me. My thoughts were suddenly interrupted by the sound of a familiar voice. "I was told I might find you here."

I quickly turned around to find Tom standing behind me. I leapt up and held him tight, once again I cried.

Tom explained he had revisited Secret Dreams in the hope of seeing Sal to find out where I was. He wanted to speak to me face-to-face to explain everything. As he hadn't heard from me, he wasn't sure that I would want to see him again, especially after letting me down.

He knew briefly what had happened to me as Sal had given him a few of the details. I asked him what had happened the day he cancelled on me.

"It was my daughter, she was ill..."

"Oh, I'm sorry to hear that. Is she ok now?"

"Yes, she's fine now, thank you. She had a burst appendix and was rushed into hospital. I thought I was going to lose her. It brought everything back; it was awful."

It was then he told me that his wife was killed in a road traffic accident five years ago. His daughter was twelve at the time and he had brought her up on his own ever since. I didn't know what to say. I felt that same pang of guilt rush through me for all the thoughts I had had about him and his wife.

. . .

We chatted till the early hours and really got to know each other. Eventually we made our way back to the hotel room and I invited him in. He kissed me in a way that he never had before. As we lay on the bed, he caressed my body with tenderness, and for the first time since we met, we made love.

As we lay side by side afterwards, I thought about how different our previous meetings had been, and although wild and exciting, nothing could compare to what I had just shared with him.

Tom turned to face me, resting his head on his hand, he tenderly kissed my lips.

"Well, Alex, you seem to have fulfilled all my fantasies. Now what about you?"

"Me?!" I said.

He nodded. "Yes, you, what are your fantasies?"

I lay back on the bed and answered, "Mine is easy."

"Really, and what is that?"

"Well, I just want to make love on the beach." He smiled at me and said, "Do you know what? I think we can just about manage that one."

I looked across at Tom and smiled. Fantasy or not, I was something I hadn't really been for a long time – happy.

Printed in Great Britain
by Amazon